G R JORDAN

Jac's Revenge

A Jac Moonshine Thriller

First published by Carpetless Publishing 2023

First edition

ISBN: 978-1-915562-48-7

This book was professionally typeset on Reedsy.
Find out more at reedsy.com

While seeking revenge, dig two graves
- one for yourself.

Douglas Horton, American
Clergyman

Contents

Foreword	iii
Acknowledgement	iv
Novels by G R Jordan	v
Chapter 01	1
Chapter 02	9
Chapter 03	18
Chapter 04	28
Chapter 05	35
Chapter 06	44
Chapter 07	51
Chapter 08	60
Chapter 09	68
Chapter 10	77
Chapter 11	86
Chapter 12	96
Chapter 13	105
Chapter 14	114
Chapter 15	122
Chapter 16	131
Chapter 17	139
Chapter 18	148
Chapter 19	156
Chapter 20	165
Chapter 21	173

Chapter 22 182
Chapter 23 190
Chapter 24 199
Read on to discover the Patrick Smythe series! 206
About the Author 209
Also by G R Jordan 211

Foreword

The events of this book are based in the fictional US city of Mannersberg, somewhere in the north of the country. The setting, persons, law enforcement agencies and companies are entirely fictitious. The author distinctly does not recommend the actions of the protagonist as a template for life!

Acknowledgement

To Ken, Jean, Colin, Evelyn, and Rosemary for your work in bringing this novel to completion, your time and effort is deeply appreciated.

Novels by G R Jordan

Jac Moonshine Thrillers

1. Jac's Revenge
2. Jac for the People

The Highlands and Islands Detective series (Crime)

1. Water's Edge
2. The Bothy
3. The Horror Weekend
4. The Small Ferry
5. Dead at Third Man
6. The Pirate Club
7. A Personal Agenda
8. A Just Punishment
9. The Numerous Deaths of Santa Claus
10. Our Gated Community
11. The Satchel
12. Culhwch Alpha
13. Fair Market Value
14. The Coach Bomber
15. The Culling at Singing Sands
16. Where Justice Fails

17. The Cortado Club
18. Cleared to Die
19. Man Overboard!
20. Antisocial Behaviour
21. Rogues' Gallery
22. The Death of Macleod - Inferno Book 1
23. A Common Man - Inferno Book 2
24. A Sweeping Darkness - Inferno Book 3
25. Dormie 5
26. The First Minister - Past Mistakes Book 1
27. The Guilty Parties - Past Mistakes Book 2
28. Vengeance is Mine - Past Mistakes Book 3
29. Winter Slay Bells

Kirsten Stewart Thrillers (Thriller)

1. A Shot at Democracy
2. The Hunted Child
3. The Express Wishes of Mr MacIver
4. The Nationalist Express
5. The Hunt for 'Red Anna'
6. The Execution of Celebrity
7. The Man Everyone Wanted
8. Busman's Holiday
9. A Personal Favour
10. Infiltrator
11. Implosion
12. Traitor

The Contessa Munroe Mysteries (Cozy Mystery)

1. Corpse Reviver
2. Frostbite
3. Cobra's Fang

The Patrick Smythe Series (Crime)

1. The Disappearance of Russell Hadleigh
2. The Graves of Calgary Bay
3. The Fairy Pools Gathering

Austerley & Kirkgordon Series (Fantasy)

1. Crescendo!
2. The Darkness at Dillingham
3. Dagon's Revenge
4. Ship of Doom

Supernatural and Elder Threat Assessment Agency (SETAA) Series (Fantasy)

1. Scarlett O'Meara: Beastmaster

to two in the morning, and the docks are quiet, except for the occasional ship that's being loaded. Most of the boats, however, are lit up because there'll be crew on board waiting to set sail or waiting to get some shore leave.

I'm dressed in black, some stout boots just in case I have to go over any rough terrain, black trousers, tight jacket, and a black headscarf. Some people would think it makes me look like a ninja, but I'm not a ninja, although I understand martial arts. I'm actually a housewife—have been ever since I married Alan. That's my husband. He's dead, but more of that later. Suffice that you know that what I'm doing now is because of what they did to him.

As I said, my name is Deborah Jacqueline Parlor, but nobody tonight will hear me say that name. Instead, they may run into Jac Moonshine. If they hear that name, they'll probably assume it's a man. If they look closely at my figure, I'm definitely a woman. I'm not one of those girls who looks like a man in a poor light. I'm not a muscle-bound person. I have a woman's frame, and in fairness, it's in decent condition. It's in better condition than it was a few months ago, but then a few months ago, I still had Alan.

I'm also a mom, but tonight, I'm an arsonist. Inside my jacket pocket is a small bottle of what Americans might call hooch; moonshine is another term for it, but you can call it what you will. Potcheen was the term of my grandfather, but if you say that over here, it means nothing.

You may have guessed I'm in the US of A, and I came here when I was nineteen years of age. By twenty, I was married, but again, that's unimportant for tonight. What's important tonight is that the building in front of me is going to go on fire. It's owned by a man called Randazzo, who's big in the underworld here. The city of Mannersberg is not an old city, but then again, how many are truly old in America? When you come from the Emerald Isle and have spent a lot of your life on the British Isles over the Irish Sea, you understand what an old city looks like. Places that are just part of daily life and yet may have been there for over a thousand years.

Mannersberg is less than one hundred years old. It started as a small port looking to bring in whiskies from Canada. This, of course, was after Prohibition, but today it's much more than that. It has its own version of Silicon Valley, as they call it—a tech district that rivals most in the world, located on the outskirts, with many production plants. While Mannersberg sits on the coast, within fifty miles are some of the most farmed parts of this country. Vincent Manners, he built the place. His family helped it grow, but that's enough of the history lesson. It's time to get to work.

In front of me, the large, clad building is lit up from the edge of the roof by many spotlights. There's a loading bay at the rear and the occasional pallet truck is passing backwards and forwards. The night shift is on and I'm biding my time, waiting for them to all retire into the canteen at the other end of the building. I've done my homework, you see.

If I set fire to the rear, the alarms will go off and everyone in the canteen will walk straight out to the car park on the opposite side. I'm not here to kill people. I'm here to burn things, Randazzo's things. The merchandise inside is clothing, cheap clothing, though. Randazzo brings it in from other countries, illegally. Once he's had it fake-stamped, all the documentation put in place, it becomes another legitimate side of his business, and it comes here, to this warehouse. I know this because my husband used to do the accounts for him. Well, the legitimate accounts. I'm getting ahead of myself.

A siren goes off, piercing the night. It's higher pitched in tone than the occasional foghorn you might hear from the boats, indicating they're at anchor or on the move. I've never been one for all those signals. I can see the staff walking away and I wait for another five minutes till everything's clear. From watching the place two nights before, I know that the break is thirty-five minutes; they must get five minutes to get there and get back. Looking at it now, you wouldn't believe the place was open except for the lights. And the rear door has been left ajar, so I pick up the first canister of fuel and lug it over towards the rear door of the warehouse.

Tonight's cold, and I wish I was wearing a big fleece jacket. The black jacket I wear is tight on my body. That's because it's easier to fight that way, easier to keep everyone else away from me. Long, swinging coats and, heaven forbid, capes just get in the way. The leggings I'm wearing as well are tight, but my hair is sitting underneath a wig. My fake hair, however, is coming out the back of the wrap-around mask that I've fashioned. It's important they think a blonde is doing this if I get seen. I'm a brunette and the number of times I want to change my hair color makes putting my head in a sink and dying it unrealistic. Wigs are better even if they do make you sweat a bit. Not a bad thing on this cold night.

The canister's carried just above the ground not just because it's heavy, but to keep it from being scraped along the ground. Once I have the canister by the door, I run into the rear of the warehouse, glancing around, but there's no one there. I undo the top of the jerrycan and haul it up onto my shoulders before leaning forward and allowing the liquid to pour over a mass of jumpers.

I walk back and forth, controlling the canister, letting the liquid drop, and trying to ignore that pungent but intoxicating smell that's filtering in through the material over my nose. Having completed my task, I walk back with the empty canister, set it on the ground, and bring over the next one. I don't have that long. The canister's up on my shoulder and I'm pouring more of the liquid.

As I'm finishing the fourth trip and the last of the liquid is falling out, I hear movement. I set down the canister and hide behind an extensive set of boxes, probably containing the packed jumpers. An old man walks in through the opening, dressed in a white shirt and black trousers. He's got a radio and a gun and for some reason at this time of night, he's sporting sunglasses. Clearly, he has no idea how to be a security guard, but I see him go for his radio.

I race out from behind the boxes, sprinting hard. Before the man has the communication device to his mouth, I've grabbed it, twisted his arm and allowed the radio to drop to the ground. I take his hand up behind his back, followed by the other one, and grab a pair of handcuffs from his belt. I soon have his wrists locked together behind his back, and I deliver a blow into the rear of his head.

It's firm. I want to knock him out, but I don't want to kill him. He just looks so frail. I watch his head slump over to the side and drag him out to the edge of the building. I can't take him all the way out. I don't want him to be seen too quickly, but at least where he is, by the time he wakes up, he should be able to get clear of the building.

I walk back inside, take out the matches, and lob them one after another into the fuel-soaked clothing before me. They erupt in a ball of flame and I have to step back from the heat

He's unconscious, but they'll find him there.

There are now firefighters running round the side of the building, and one shouts over at me. I ignore them, turn, and run as hard as I can over to the water's edge at the pier. It's one step, a large jump, and I hit the water feet first.

You're maybe thinking, *why didn't she dive?* It's mainly because I'm rubbish at it, but I can swim, and with powerful strokes in the dark, I swim along the pier's edge, going underneath it intermittently.

As I clamber out at an abandoned dock further down, I can still sniff the cloy smell of burned fabric. I can still taste the acrid fumes. I scramble up steps that lead from the water and steal back to the car, mission accomplished for tonight. My only concern is I won't get to see Randazzo's face.

I sit in the car, unwrap my head cover, take off the wig, undo the jacket and the leggings, and change into some light jeans and a t-shirt. From there, I dump everything else into the trunk before starting the car and heading for home. It's been a good night, even if I am damp with a car to clear up, but I think I need to take you back. I think you need to understand just what it was I was dealing with.

Chapter 02

I started somewhere in the middle, so I think we'll go further back. You're probably wondering what makes a housewife become an arsonist. Well, arson's probably the least of it, but you don't know why, and you don't know the whens and the wherefores, so let's go back a bit. I've told you already, my name's Deborah Jacqueline Parlor. I'm a housewife to Alan Parlor. Not that I was too stupid or too dumb to get a job, but Alan made enough money, and he gave me time. Time to do my acting, which I am very fond of. Time to work out, time to do my martial arts, and time to do all these by nipping around on my little green scooter.

Back in the days before Jac Moonshine was even a thing, I would tend to the home, take care of the social lives of myself and Alan, and our daughter Kelly, but that's probably best told after I tell you the juicy bit.

Alan was an accountant, but every day I knew him, Alan was calm. Calculating, yes, but always calm. Nothing fazed Alan until that day. I had been rehearsing for the amateur drama, *Romeo and Juliet*. They'd cast me as Juliet. It was ridiculous, because, well, I'm old for that part. I was one of the younger ones amongst the actors, which says more about our troop than about my acting skills.

I'd been looking at makeup and costumes upstairs, deciding what to wear, when I heard him storm in downstairs. It got the prickles up on my neck as soon as I heard him come in. He never slammed the door, so I marched downstairs with the dressing gown around me, having taken off the other costumes previously. It's a nice three-quarter number that he bought me. Real silk, too, but as I came down the stairs wearing it, he barely looked at me.

That wasn't Alan. Alan was an attentive husband. When he came in, he gave me a kiss, even when he wasn't feeling like it. Even if he had a rubbish day, Alan always came over and said, "Hello." Instead, he stormed through to the kitchen.

I knew something was up as well because he bypassed the coffee straight into the whiskey. I saw the glass he poured. It wasn't a shot, or a half inch. There was at least three inches of whiskey in that tumbler, and it wasn't a whiskey tumbler either. He downed it in two goes. I think he was aiming to do it in one, but it caught him. There was a bit of coughing and spluttering before the second section of the drink went down.

I remember our daughter passed by. She was eighteen, and she said to him, "What the fuck, Da?" His left arm swung around, caught her with the back of his hand, right in the cheek. He'd hit nobody in our family. He'd never even threatened it.

"Language," he said.

"What on earth, Alan?" I cried. "Alan, what on earth? When did you ever?"

He spun round, the empty glass in one hand. "Don't, Debbie," he said. "Don't. She doesn't get to use that language."

"And you don't get to smack her across the face. When did you ever do that? When have you ever hit a woman?"

I saw him shake. No, it was a tremble, genuine fear. He put the glass back down, poured another inch or two of whiskey, and downed it again. Kelly was sobbing, and I walked over to her to hold her, but she ran off up the stairs.

I rounded on him. "Alan, what on earth?"

"At least you didn't swear like she did. She doesn't get to talk to me like that. She doesn't get to . . ."

"Alan, enough," I said suddenly and then stepped slowly closer to him, putting my hand up to the back of his neck. If he was tense, you could feel it there.

It didn't feel like he was tense. It felt like he was about to explode. It felt like Alan's knobs had all been turned up to three hundred percent. He was ready to overload, but he was also reeling. But not with anger. With terror.

"What's the matter?" I asked him.

"I don't know," he said. "I don't know. I need to talk to Eddie. I need to sort it out."

The "Eddie" he was referring to is Eddie Tumbler. Now, Eddie works for Alan's boss, Randazzo. I think I told you, Randazzo is into some nasty stuff. Eddie works on that side, and he's the one that tells Alan when to come and see Randazzo. Alan's always been a brilliant accountant because he's working on legit things. He was happy to take Randazzo's money.

I said to him, "Is it not risky getting involved with the likes of those people?" and Alan said he was just the accountant. He wasn't working on the side where they had to hide anything, wasn't working on the side where anything was illegal. He was just covering off the legitimate side of the business. Therefore, he would be safe.

Now, when he first told me that, I was all "very good," but I found out afterwards that even working on the legitimate side, these guys, well, they have an attitude, and a lifestyle, and their attitude to women especially is not good. I think their wives are housewives. They don't like them working elsewhere. It's wrong to them. It's like, "Why should the women have to fend for themselves?" It was almost an insult if your wife worked.

I remember once talking about a job, and Alan was, "No, don't. It's too much of a hassle. It will not work out." If I'm truthful, I'm not someone who wants to work, so I just occupied my time with Kelly when she came along, and all the things that I wanted to do. But I'm digressing now.

I took Alan over to the couch in the front room, and I started rubbing the back of his neck again. I told him to calm down. It took time, but he did, but I still had to keep my hands on his neck and on his knee. The knee was the worst. It was jumping like he had Parkinson's. Back then, I didn't know all about Randazzo's illegal operations. I'd seen some numbers that Alan had run through because he'd been working in the lounge, so I knew the man was big in terms of the city and in what finances he had at his disposal. But all Alan would say was, "I got it wrong. I got it wrong."

I told him that things could be corrected, but he said they couldn't, they simply couldn't, and then he stared up at me.

"You need to pack our bags, Debbie," he said. "We need to go. We'll need to get out of here. I'll book a flight. We've probably got a couple of days, but we'll book a flight. I'll talk to Eddie before then. See if it'll calm down."

He leaned in on me and I could hear him praying. Alan barely prayed. We went to church, of course we did, and we'd sit there, the pristine family. Except that Kelly never really did. She was just a typical teenager.

When he said, "Pack our bags," I stood up. I felt I needed to get his attention.

"What the hell, Alan? Pack our bags? This is my life."

"No," said Alan. "I am. Kelly is. This is just stuff. All this is just stuff. We can go. We can leave. We'll find somewhere. Why don't you go back to Ireland? Why don't we all go to Ireland?"

"Ireland?" I blurted. "I haven't been to Ireland since I was a teen. Why would I be going back to Ireland? I came here to be with you. This is where we made a life."

"We can make it again," he said. He was earnest.

"If we're going to travel," I said, "and you can't get a flight, we can get in the car and we can go. We'll need to get some food and things. I'll need to pack up."

"I know," he said. "I know." He went quiet, then said, "Why? Why did I do that?"

"You're under stress," I said. "It's okay. You won't do it again." I kissed him on the cheek, but he was so tense.

"It's not fair," he said. "It's just not fair."

"How much trouble are you in?" I asked.

"I'm not sure. It was Viktor Kozlov."

"I don't know Viktor Kozlov."

"You don't want to know Viktor Kozlov, but I dropped a big one with him. It was just a casual look, but he took it completely the wrong way. Kozlov's a big player with Randazzo, and I think he thinks I insulted Kozlov. You don't do that with these people. I'm just an accountant. Ultimately, I'm nobody. I'm not part of that family, I'm not part of their group. I'm just a guy that does the money. There's plenty more like me."

"There's nobody like you," I said. "Will Eddie be able to make everyone see sense?"

"I don't know. Eddie's . . . well, Eddie's as much like him as any of them."

"Go upstairs," I said. "Go upstairs and sort out what you can. Sort out your daughter. Okay? I'll start packing, then we'll tell her. She won't be happy, but that doesn't matter."

"It's been twenty years that I've worked for him. Twenty years, Debbie."

I nodded. "I know," I said. "I remember him being here the first time you brought him to the house. I never liked him. I never liked him, Alan. He was grabby. I told you he felt my backside the first time he came in."

"I know," said Alan, "but the money was good. I was just starting out. It's given us everything."

"It has, but sounds like it's time to go."

I pushed Alan up the stairs to talk to Kelly. As soon as he was out of view, I could feel myself shaking. I didn't know then who Randazzo and his people really were, but I knew they weren't good. I knew the police had been after them, but I didn't understand fully how big he was.

I continued to be a good wife, though. I packed suitcases. I got us ready to go. We were going to the grocery store to pick up a few things. Alan was going to see if he could get a meeting with Eddie that night. If he didn't and if Eddie wasn't speaking, we were going to get in the car and drive south till we got to Florida or somewhere, and then get a flight out of the country. Maybe go over to Ireland. Even if they were nasty people, I doubted they would come all the way to Ireland. Ireland's got its own ways and means, though I left that behind a long time ago. But my father and grandfather are still alive over there and they would know.

I nearly cried when I walked into the room and saw Alan

hugging Kelly. The two of them were always close. She preferred Alan to me and that wasn't just from the teenage years. They say that about the teenage years, don't they? Girl becomes almost a woman, and you can't have two women running a house. You clash. Well, you do. She never clashed with her dad. Not in that way.

One thing I understood, standing at the door of Kelly's room, was that Kelly realized what her father was saying to her. She probably understood the players less than I did, but she understood he was probably going to take a beating for it. Something like that. I don't think she imagined what was coming. I didn't imagine what was coming. I was scared, but we had a plan. We had a plan and everything was going to be okay that day because Alan was going to talk to Eddie, and then we'd be gone. Tomorrow wouldn't be a problem. Today, we just had to get sorted.

An hour and a half later, we all piled into the station wagon to go down to the grocery store. I'd used it for the last twenty years and I remember the checkout assistant was Mary. Mary had been a seventeen-year-old girl when I'd first gone in. I was barely a few years older. We chatted and for a while she'd even been at the drama with me. She was a sad case because she'd gotten pregnant; he didn't stick around, and she struggled to raise her baby. I'd see her every now and again, but she went right off me when she found out who Alan worked for. Several people did. It was usually people with less. The higher up you got in society, in the city, they never seemed to mind.

Back then, I never fathomed it. I never questioned it. I was the housewife. I looked after the family. I made everything right at home. Alan dealt with the outside. Mary gave me the cold shoulder when we went shopping, and as we pushed the trolley out into the car park by the station wagon, there was a black car at the far end. It drove down along the road, stopping briefly as an old woman marched out in front of it. We'd got about eight bags into the trunk at that point, and I was putting some more in when I saw the car speed up. Alan recognized it, for he turned around as the window rolled down and went to talk to the person in the passenger seat. I turned, as did Kelly, both of us staring.

Until that point in my life, I had never really encountered proper violence. I had never encountered a serious threat, anything more than a mild thug, but right then, my life changed. I could bore you with all the gory details. I could tell you about how Alan's head snapped back. I could tell you about his body being thrown onto the trunk of our car, so his shoulders rested on it afterwards. I won't tell you where his head ended. I will tell you that Kelly screamed, as did I.

The world spun after that gunshot. Detective Frogg came along, told us it was a shotgun right in Alan's face. It was people Alan knew. Frogg made a big deal of the fact they'd shot him in the face. He said he knew my husband did accounts for Randazzo, and he tried to ask questions about what I knew, tried to find out if there was a connection. I didn't know. Kelly didn't know. Not then.

Every night I went to sleep wondering if I'd see that again. The last memory of my husband was of him being horribly, brutally disfigured by friends. I remember the blood hitting me, splattering Kelly. When they took us to the police station, they had us change clothes because . . . well, I think they took them to forensics, and I told them to burn the clothes afterwards.

As we sat later that night with Detective Frogg in front of

us, I asked him, could he get these men? Would he be able to deal with them? He said to me that somebody would need to inform on Randazzo. Someone would need to break cover and rank. He asked me if I would break cover and rank. I told him I would, but I had nothing to break with.

I checked Alan's accounts and dealings in the weeks that followed. He was clean as a whistle. He had done nothing illegal, but Randazzo had him killed. Had him killed for Viktor Kozlov, all because Alan gave a look he didn't like. I still to this day don't know what he did, and frankly, I don't care. If your friends can do that to you, they are not friends.

I pulled a security guard from the fire because he was an innocent. He was just doing his job. It was a normal job, part of Randazzo's clean operations. The man would've applied for it like anyone else, but that day changed me. If Frogg had said, "Yes, we can get them; we know how to go after him," I probably would've just let him, but he didn't. He said they probably wouldn't get him.

I thought you should know this because this is the day that made Jac Moonshine. Not the day that made me. That was the day I got married. But the day Alan died, Jac Moonshine was born.

Chapter 03

You might think that was it. A husband shot down in front of me and my daughter and that's what drove me to do it. That was it. I said Jac Moonshine was born then, and she was, but she wasn't kiln-fired, shall we say. The clay had been spun; the pot had been made to a degree, but it still had to be put in the kiln, and it had to be glazed and finished. For that to happen, it took the funeral.

Because of the people that Alan worked for, the funeral was covered. I found out later that it's how they worked within their group. Alan was family to them. I don't know about you, but my family never turned around and shot each other in the face. We fought . . . and we called each other names back in Ireland; sometimes I got a skelp on the backside for having done something that my parents thought was wrong, but never did they haul me out and blow my face off.

I apologize if the way I talk about Alan's death offends you, but I have to talk about it that way. I must talk about it as if it's just some freak and weird thing, because if I sit down and think about it, I just fall apart. I just curl up and weep and Debbie comes out. I guess Debbie died that day along with Alan—certainly a large part of Debbie. Debbie was that good little housewife. But Debbie was not put upon. When I was Debbie, I loved it. I loved having free time. I loved bringing up Kelly. I was someone who enjoyed motherhood, who relished looking after her man.

I ran the house. Alan ran outside the house, and we worked as a team. I owned Alan, and Alan owned me. We firmly believed that, and meant that in every aspect of life, finances, household, intimacy, everything. We had respect for each other. The man that walked in that day shaking, that was not Alan. Sometimes I think they killed him quickly because he knew it could go that way. He was a flight risk. I didn't realize that Alan understood what had happened to other people within that so-called family.

Of course, the people outside of the family who crossed them usually ended up a lot worse. Now, you're thinking, how could you end up a lot worse? In truth, they probably thought they were being kind to Alan and us. Randazzo paid for Alan's funeral, and it was ridiculous. He didn't ask me what flowers I wanted on Alan's coffin. Instead, he paid for this massive thing that said, "Dad." Kelly never called him Dad. It was Da, always Da, and Kelly never would've chosen those flowers—too bright. Alan didn't like that sort of thing. Alan liked stuff that was demure. Kelly knew that. I knew that. Randazzo knew nothing.

There was a lineup of people I'd never met. They were probably from the family, all hauled out, the gangster network, all knowing what had happened to Alan. He'd done something out of turn, or at least allegedly, and for that, he died. I know in the Old Testament, it talks about taking out a child and stoning them because of their disobedience, but we're past that. I struggled with that funeral, and it wasn't the day I laid

Alan to rest. I did that simply on my own at his grave. A very cold day, but on that other day I said goodbye to my husband.

Kelly, however, thought the funeral should be about us, about me and her, and how we felt about her Da and remembering him. Instead, Randazzo got Eddie Tumbler to do the eulogy. He knew nothing about Alan. There was nothing in it that spoke of his character, spoke of the father he was. Kelly would've spoken well. She loved him that much.

At the lineup, after we had put Alan into the ground, Randazzo was the first to walk past us. He shook my hand, telling me how he was going to make sure I was looked after, but Kelly went for him. She was dressed in black, and the fists flew. Randazzo is a large man, just over six feet, wide as a horse. A bit of a belly; mind, he's not in great shape—probably all the booze, sex, women, and whatever the heck else they get up to.

I had to grab her. At her father's funeral, I had to stop Kelly from beating the man who ordered his death. Kelly didn't know it was him specifically then, but he was the head of the crime syndicate, so he was getting the blame. In front of all the others who were following to give their condolences, Randazzo told me in my ear to "Get a hold of that fucking bitch, because if she does that again, I won't be responsible for what I do to her."

He'd never been so insulted. "She should be a good little woman like you," he told me. The fire that burned within me was immeasurable. The kiln was at a temperature I'd never seen, and the pot was fixed to such a degree it would never break again.

One of the last people to pass us by was a man called Daniel, Alan's junior accountant. He was only twenty-three, a very likable chap, and Alan always spoke of him highly. He was very genuine when he said he was sorry. By now, Randazzo and a lot of the others had left, and Daniel said something he probably shouldn't have. He told me it was very harsh on Alan. Because the others had disappeared, I asked him what he meant.

You can see fear in people. Sometimes it's the body that shakes; sometimes it's the eyes. They widen and Daniel's nearly exploded that day. To be fair to him, I think he felt he owed me. I think he wanted to look after me, to do for me. Probably the best thing he could have done was not tell me, but out of no malice, but simply trying to do something for me, he said that Viktor Kozlov took offense at Alan's smile one night. It wasn't a word. It wasn't a remark to Kozlov. It was Alan's smile. Alan's beautiful smile was what Kozlov took offense at.

Right there, I decided to kill him. Right there, I decided to kill the whole damn lot of them.

Daniel continued quietly. He said that Randazzo was told by Kozlov to whack Alan, to kill him because of that smile; otherwise, Kozlov was going to pull out of a major drug deal. Randazzo's men were the people who did it, the people that Alan sat alongside in their meetings, the ones he had been to the weddings of.

Oh, I remember it. We had to go every time one of their bloody children got married and I had to turn up, not in what I wanted to wear, but something that showed my legs and a good bit of cleavage.

I remember Alan trying to make sure I would be *presentable*. He was very subtle. I was wearing an outfit I thought was prim and wouldn't take away from the people being married or the family that was in celebration. *Go along and just be yourself, but be quiet and be to the side. Don't take over,* I thought. I can shine, you see. I was lucky. I was born with looks and a figure, but don't get me wrong. I don't look to use them despite my mother's encouragement when I was seventeen.

"Shove that chest out. Make sure you show a bit of those legs. You'll get a good husband that way." She wasn't a feminist by anyone's imagination.

I have absolutely no idea why my mother thought that would bring me a good husband. She was quirky. Maybe she thought it would bring somebody with money because we had little.

I went to those funerals, dressed in something a bit more, or rather, less than I thought I would wear. Alan said to me, "Why are you wearing that? You have a better figure than that, love. You should show a wee bit more," but he said it with a tone of sadness.

Alan loved me in jeans. Alan loved me in a long skirt or a large dress. Alan loved me with nothing on. Alan loved me whatever the heck way I was and he would never tell me what to wear. In some ways, he was a typical husband.

"How do I look?"

"Great."

I usually had to ask Kelly for the real opinion. In saying that, Alan probably thought I looked great.

Randazzo's men did it. They were the ones in the car. That was why Alan knew them and he told them to shoot him in the face. This may not seem important to you; somebody puts a gun to your head, front or back, what does it matter? Pull the trigger, the same thing happens. But it was a mark of disrespect.

This is why I don't get these families and remember, they say they're a family. I don't get it. Business comes before family. If somebody's out of line or if somebody's done something, even if they're not that aware of it, what's the best way to tell you? You bring somebody in, you're responsible for them. If they turn out to be a bad egg, well, you go down too, but because you're family, they'll shoot you in the back of the head. You won't see it coming. How generous is that? You won't even know. The other one, they'll take away somewhere. They'll beat the living daylights out of them, torture them to who knows what degree, and then they'll kill them. But hey, at least a family member died without knowing about it.

I asked Daniel for more than that. I asked Daniel for details, but he said he couldn't. He said he feared for his life and he asked me never to repeat what I said. Of course, I didn't. I couldn't. Daniel was a good kid. Daniel tried to help me. There was no way I could run to the police and say, "But Daniel said. I have evidence. I have a witness." Probably would've been second hand, anyway. Daniel never said if he was in the room or if it was rumors he'd heard.

One unexpected person at the funeral was Detective Frogg. He came past and said sorry after everyone else had left. I'm not sure he wanted to be in amongst them. Maybe he feared for his own life. Maybe he was all ears trying to find out what had happened. He was never one of them. In fairness to Frogg, as inadequate as the police force was, Frogg was never working for Randazzo. I think he genuinely wanted to protect me. I think he feared what life was going to throw at me.

After the funeral and a brief delay of maybe half an hour for us to get back, I had to entertain everyone at the house. Randazzo was there again, but it wasn't him who came to me. Maybe he was upset. Maybe he kept away from Kelly and me because he knew Kelly might go for him, for she was still like thunder, and then he would have to do something. Maybe he saw that as being generous, looking out for us. When I started this path, I never understood their mindset. Where I am now, I can follow it, but I'll never understand it. My mindset's much simpler: you killed my husband, and you killed him for a smile. You wrecked my daughter's life. You wrecked mine.

They tell you at the church to forgive and forget, but it's not that simple. I would never be free of those bastards and what happened next told me that.

I was in the kitchen. I think I was going to bring out some soup that I had made for the funeral. They were all hanging around my lounge, my veranda, making a mockery of my home, all sitting and saying what a kind soul Alan was, even those who had murdered him. I didn't know who, but that meant everyone got tarnished with the same brush.

I was in the kitchen ladling the soup into a different container to carry through when Eddie Tumbler came in. Eddie's shorter than Randazzo. He's got a scar along the side of his mouth. He walked up behind me. Without asking, he put his hands on my shoulders; he rubbed them.

"Must be a hell of a day for you, Debbie," he said. "Losing your man, losing your protection must be scary, especially after the way Randazzo chewed you out. You'll need to take Kelly in hand. Maybe you need a powerful man to do that."

I said nothing. To say I was vulnerable is the understatement of the year. I was almost at their mercy. He threatened to kill my daughter. Randazzo threatened her after he blew off her father's head and I had to restrain her, apologize to him for it. I tell you these things because you need to understand where I come from. I'm not a bad person. The police hadn't the means or skills to bring about justice. They wouldn't solve this, and I certainly couldn't live with it not being dealt with.

Eddie Tumbler continued to rub my shoulders, but then the hands slipped down. They were on the edges of my shoulders, then my arms and down to my hips.

"I can protect you," he said. "It's early days, so I won't force any issues," he said. "We'll give it time, then you and I, well, we could get together. If you're my woman, Randazzo won't touch you. I can keep that girl of yours in check."

His hands went onto my hips, squeezing them and pulling himself towards me. There was a set of knives off to my left, and I wanted to plunge them into him. I wanted to grab them and stab him repeatedly. Not in the chest, in the face. I wanted to chop his hands off so he could never touch another woman again, and I almost lost it. I almost did it, but what kept me from doing it wasn't the fact that I would destroy myself. I would become like them. Oh, no, never. What stopped me was they would take me away or deal with me before I got near Randazzo and Kozlov.

As he felt my hips and then one hand pulled up my blouse and his hand went across my belly, the pot in the kiln was finished. This was the glaze going on top. His hand went higher and I won't describe what he did because some would take it as being some sexual thrill almost when it wasn't. It was the opposite. It was gross. I am a woman who likes physical contact. With Alan and me, it was never a problem. I loved it. He did too. It was ours. He owned me and I owned him, and this man came in and said he owned me without even asking.

I couldn't go to the cops with this. That would have ended up in probably a severe beating for me and maybe Kelly's death, because she would have gone off the handle. She might not get on with her mother, but she'll defend me to the hilt if somebody else attacks me because we're family, not like these lecherous, evil failures of men.

It was Daniel, thank God, who rescued me. He opened the door to the kitchen with a simple, "Can I help?" I think Eddie must have smiled at him. The hands retracted, and he slipped out the door. Daniel saw me tucking my blouse back in.

It says a lot about the character of the man that he didn't walk away in horror. He didn't think that this was me trying to establish a new man in my life or trying to worm my way into money or even protection. He simply walked up to me and whispered, "Are you okay?"

Daniel taught me an important lesson that day, and one I carried with me, and one that probably saved the life of that guard in the blazing inferno of a warehouse. Not everything Randazzo touched turned evil. There were inherently good people out there just stuck working with the slime of the earth. Daniel was one of them.

I vowed to keep those people safe from whatever I was going to do, but as for everyone else connected with Randazzo and Kozlov, if you were part of the filth, you would get cleaned up.

I stood pouring the rest of the soup and thought to myself, *What do I need to do this?* Understand there was no decision. I didn't ponder whether I could do it, whether I could go after Randazzo and Kozlov and end what they were. Oh, no, I was doing it. All I needed to do was to understand what I needed to be, what else I needed around me, and how to do it.

I threw up that night thinking about what Eddie Tumbler did to me. It was probably a good thing, purging the stench of him. Kelly asked me why I was sick. I couldn't tell her. She had to be protected from it. She had to be kept out. She had my fiery head. She could rage and go for things just the same as I. I just had the years to understand the consequences of such actions were not what we wanted.

Yes, the pot was glazed that day. It was ready.

Chapter 04

During the next step, I got something wrong. I pushed Kelly away because I had to make plans. I decided to go on holiday. For the weeks after the funeral, until I went on holiday, I understood I was keeping Kelly at a distance. It was with the best of intentions, as I couldn't involve her, and she was spinning out of control. I could have sat down with her and told her what I was going to do. I didn't because she would want to be involved. She would have wanted to kill them as much as I did.

Kelly had trouble in school. She was drinking too much, and I decided I needed her to get out of my life for a week or two. I was running around after her trying to clear up messes, attempting to deal with it, and I wasn't. I was just pushing her away. I was dealing with the rubbish that came alongside it, not dealing with her.

I sent her back to Ireland. She had friends over there because we'd visited several times in her life and I thought it was the best thing for her. I still don't think it was bad for her, but she didn't have her mom. She'd lost her Da and the first thing I did was take her mom away.

Well, Debbie was gone. That perfect housewife, that person

who found her perfect mate and wanted to make it work, she had disappeared. I think she got buried in the ground with Alan. This vengeful wreck came out, and that's why I went on holiday, not to get rid of the vengefulness but to get rid of the wreck. If I was going to take on these people, I needed to learn how to handle a gun. I could fight. I knew my martial arts, and I was damn good at it. I had accumulated twenty years of practice, twenty years of working hard three times a week. Oh, I can handle myself. In fact, that was often the hard bit.

When Eddie Tumbler grabbed me from behind, I could have put an elbow through his head. I could have grabbed him by the hair, put him on the table, and hammered him repeatedly. I wouldn't have needed those knives. I'd have broken his jaw and then every bone in that face.

But I would've blown it all. In some ways, I'm thankful for the discipline I learned in my martial arts sessions. I was disciplined, being what they wanted me to be at their weddings, to help Alan, to keep our family safe. Did that mean I had to show a bit more leg than I wanted? Yes. Did that mean I had to appear as they wanted me? Yes, but that meant I could do it in those moments at the funeral. I could keep the cover established.

I realized quickly that if I was going to take on Randazzo and Kozlov and bring them down, there was a heck of a big organization to take on. I didn't know all the key figures. I remember being away in Europe, in Portugal with a whiteboard on a wall and writing up who I knew and doing research to find out who else was involved with Randazzo. Kozlov was harder. I knew I'd have to bring him to Randazzo. I couldn't disappear off to Columbia to perform a killing. I knew nothing about Colombia.

It's amazing what you can learn from other countries. I found a man who taught me how to use a firearm. Jorge taught me how to use it, and for a month, every afternoon, I went to him and practiced. I got better. Don't get me wrong; I didn't end up a crack shot, but if you were less than twenty yards away, I'd hit you and I'd hit you well enough to follow up and kill you with a better shot.

He taught me how to be detached, how not to have anger pumping in my veins, how to be relaxed when I shot, because the weapons would kick and I have to be prepared for that. How to think, how to turn and see what I was shooting before that trigger went. I thought about Daniel. I wouldn't want to burst into a room and find I'd taken him out.

Jorge was a gentleman. He must have been in his seventies, although I never asked, and every afternoon getting close to mealtime, which for him was around seven, this little old lady would appear. I think she was his wife, not his mother. Jorge would thank me and tell me to stay safe until he saw me the next day. He would tell me about the wonderful cooking of this woman and how this woman was what mattered in his life. It brought back a lot of memories of Alan.

I learned to fire a gun. I also spent hours in front of a mirror, dressing up, putting on wigs, applying makeup, changing my appearance. This would be critical. What I couldn't do was appear in front of these goons as Debbie. If they found out I was Debbie, Kelly was dead. It was a harsh but simple truth. By doing this, I was putting Kelly at risk, but there was no way I could keep Kelly in Ireland while I was attempting it. It would seem strange that Kelly was away. They wouldn't have liked it either. It was difficult enough getting permission to go on this holiday. I remember because Eddie came round, and I'd had to let him, well, enjoy himself a bit. Is that the best way to put it? My reaction was everything opposite to that.

I know some people will think they couldn't do that, but their husbands hadn't died in front of their face. Inside, there was a hardness that had grown in me, a hardness that was mixed with anger and rage. What impressed me was how I controlled it, how this outer shell held it all in. When I saw Kelly, I saw myself except for the wisdom of years, except for the discipline, except for the ability to understand the consequences of not holding it in.

I became extremely focused, but also in Portugal, I cried. I went to bed every night in tears. I wept for Alan. One day, I turned up for my gun practice and Jorge said to me, "Why do your eyes look so dark?"

I said that I'd been bereaved and wanted to just pass that off, but Jorge said no. He said he wanted to understand my grief. I told him he couldn't. What could I do? Find someone he loved and shoot them in front of his face.

The next day, he was at my door several hours before I would go to practice my shooting with him. He asked if he could stay near me. He didn't ask where I went, he didn't ask what I did, but I let him follow me. Behind the little house I'd rented, there was a small brook, and on the far side of it, I'd erected a headstone. I had made it out of small stones that were lying about but I had put a plaque on it and the plaque said, "Alan Parlor, dearly beloved husband and father. Taken before his time."

I watched Jorge read it and then he read the bit that I'd put at the bottom, "Vengeance is mine."

He looked at me and smiled. "This isn't a quote from God," he said. I looked at him, a bit bemused. "This is a quote from you, isn't it?" I nodded. "Can you tell me about it?" he asked. "I want to understand so that you will be in control when you fire a weapon."

I think it was three days later that I said to him I wanted to go to a little taverna somewhere where we could chat but quiet, somewhere where we wouldn't be overheard. We sat and had a meal of chicken and rice and afterwards, he ordered drinks and I sat and told him everything.

At the end, I said to him, "Can I trust you with this? Otherwise, I'm going to have to kill you." He laughed at that. He said he was the instructor with the gun. He was no—he asked how the Americans said it—freshman?

Then he said to me, "I'm seventy-nine." Man, the guy didn't look it. He said to me he would take it to the grave. He wouldn't tell his wife, but he'd tell his wife I was special. I was to be looked after.

I dined with him several times after that at her invite and never once did she ask me. Jorge taught me how to be cool, taught me not to see Randazzo there, taught me not what I had been doing, firing in rage. He taught me how to humble myself, taught me how to push away the emotion so I could react quicker, shoot better. I thank God I found him because he changed things.

He came another morning and asked if he could come inside. I let him and I showed him the makeup, the wigs. I got changed into various outfits for him. I also told him about Eddie Tumbler and what he did to me at that funeral. I told him about Randazzo and how he had got Alan to tell me to dress differently. He told me he understood what I was doing, but he also asked did I have anyone else. I told him about Kelly. That was when he looked worried. He told me he had to go off and think about it.

We couldn't practice that day. I walked along the beach later on and spotted him at a shack bar. He was drinking and thinking. At six the next morning, there was a rap on the door. I had gone to bed with a bottle of wine, trying to chase away the memories that hurt and keep the ones of Alan I wanted. They always intermixed. I didn't get to see things the way I wanted. I opened the door to him, and he told me to get dressed.

We walked along the beach to that shack where he had been drinking the day before. He ordered coffee, and he said to me, "You are a disguise." He said it was great that I would try to be a multitude of people to keep Kelly safe.

He said the one thing that they do to us, to those that they hurt, is they produce fear. They drive fear into their enemies. Fear is a destructive thing. He said I couldn't fear them. They needed to fear me. He said I needed to be on the outside of what was driving me on the inside. I had told him what was driving me, had told him how I felt; I told him of the rage.

He said to me, "Make a costume. Make it yourself, something, an identity." I had planned to hit Randazzo's organization from here, there, and wherever in a multitude of disguises, so he wouldn't have a clue who it was, but Jorge said no.

He said, "Make it a figure that will scare him. Make it a figure that will come to haunt him." The other thing he said was, "Leave a calling card. Make sure each time, even if he doesn't see you, he knows it's you." I nodded. Jorge was right. He said that I should tell him who I was to be that afternoon. He told me not to leave the shack, and he left money behind the bar for more coffee, more wine, or whatever I wanted. He said, "Don't leave until you know."

I thought it needed to be something personal. Randazzo's

men always knew me as Debbie, but Debbie was dead. Jacqueline was my middle name. The thing about my middle name was the only person who called me Jacqueline was my mother. Except that Alan did it, but in private, in those intimate moments and in those moments when we were just us. Alan called me Jac. He said Jac was always strong, Jac was always there for him, Jac was the steel behind the family. He said he felt safe because Jac was with him. He felt loved because of Jac. He felt like a man because of Jac.

I decided it was time for the rest of the world to meet Jac. But you just can't call yourself Jac. It sounded rubbish. Moonshine. I would call myself Jac Moonshine because they wouldn't get it. I needed a calling card. It needed to be something personal, something that they couldn't link to me, but which clearly meant something personal. Well, now you know about Jac; the Moonshine is for another time.

Chapter 05

I know what you're thinking—neat little backstory. Trained yourself up. No problem, off we go. Well, this isn't the movies. It doesn't work quite like that. Information was quite hard to find and Alan was always on the good side of Randazzo's operation. Well, when I say good, I mean legitimate. Legitimate is the correct word, isn't it? Legitimate doesn't mean something is good; it just means you can't get arrested for it. Ask a politician; they'll know what I mean.

I came back from the holiday, or rather, training camp as I looked on it, ready to get a firearm and start storming the place. I'd find where Randazzo's goons hung out; I'd take down his operation. Then it struck me. I remember distinctly when I realized.

I'd come back from the holiday and got an invitation over to Patsy Seymour's. Now, Patsy's one of those lovely people, genuinely good heart, but just interferes too much in everybody's business. She wanted me over to see how I was, to make sure I was okay in a slightly patronizing way, but I can't fault people like that. They're decent. They just try a little too hard.

I was sitting in her front room, which has a sofa with a

gorgeous floral pattern. I don't know how she pulled that one off. I think they look drab, old hat normally . . . but not Patsy's. She's got a real eye for it.

So, we're sitting having a cup of coffee with two of the other ladies in the social circle whom I'm not particularly friends with. The trouble is Patsy knows everybody. I used to find this with her. You'd be sitting in a conversation and then realize that the two women you were in with, you did not know who they were, and yet Patsy knew every detail about them. She's comparing your child to their child and giving you detail that you'd forgotten about your child, and when you look at her, you think she's such an exemplary mother. How bad am I? She doesn't mean any of this because she's genuinely trying to help.

In her defense, Patsy was one of the most genuine people after Alan died. Alan had a reputation in some ways, not as a gangster, but as someone who worked for people who weren't particularly good, and because of that, and because of who came to the funeral, many people in the neighborhood didn't respond, didn't come and help or even come to give their condolences. Patsy was there straight away. She even made some food for the return to the house after the funeral. She's particularly good at quiche.

Anyway, I'm sitting there on Patsy's floral sofa, and Patsy's waxing lyrical about some performance one of the other women's child was in, and she started talking about acting.

Now, I don't think Patsy's ever been an actor, but she said, "You need to understand what's behind the character. You need to find out what's in the depths. You can't just attack a part at the top, just what everybody sees on the outside." Then she said, "You can't neglect the outside because if that falls down, the interior of how you're portraying a character falls apart."

Now, I do not know if Patsy had any formal acting training. I don't know if she's just basing this off the latest soaps she's watched, but God bless the woman because she made me understand. I didn't need to start off reaching Randazzo's deeper organization. I couldn't. I didn't know who they were. Well, I knew *who* they were.

Eddie Tumbler was there. I'd seen a lot of the others at the funeral, but I didn't know how they worked, where they lived, where they operated out of, what illegal operations they were conducting. I had in my mind I wouldn't just kill Randazzo, I would destroy him first. I would make him understand the pain he caused. Maybe I was naïve in that, but this was not an eye for an eye. No, no. It was much more serious than that.

Pasty rambled on and, God bless her, poured me another cup of coffee, but in my mind, I was thinking through what contact Alan would've had with Randazzo. I was thinking about numbers. You see, because Alan did the legitimate side of the business, there was no need to hide it. It could be kept out front. In fact, Randazzo probably kept that side out much more than any normal trader would. He wanted people to come and look at it. He wanted people like the IRS to check it out. He wanted a clean bill of health from it. I remember giving Patsy a kiss on the cheek when we left, and I said to her, "Thank you."

"Are you all right?" she said to me. Her eyes were loaded with concern. I must be honest, it felt good to have somebody who actually gave a damn. After the falseness of the funeral, I was finally finding people around me. Jorge was great out in Portugal, but it was temporary. I would not be speaking to him again, but here, living just around the corner, was Patsy.

"Shall we go to the gym," Patsy said to me, "tomorrow morning?" She knew I liked the gym. She knew that was what I enjoyed. Patsy, God bless her. She was one of those people who'd hit the gym recreationally as an adjunct to other conversations. Patsy would stand beside the machines, somebody sweating away, running like mad, and she'd be chatting. She'd come out of the gym no fitter than she went in, but armed to the teeth with interesting tidbits about the community.

I gave her a nod, thanked her, got into the car, and drove to Alan's office. Daniel was there. After all, there was a state of transition going on. Randazzo was going to move his accounts, but things hadn't been transferred over yet. I remember being in the office where Alan had large filing cabinets. Not all records were kept electronically. A lot of them were on paper.

When I came into the office, Daniel stood up, raced over, and didn't know whether to shake my hand or give condolences again. I was reasonably well-dressed, which is unusual for me. A red skirt that flopped about close to my shins, red heels on, but not high,—after all, I wasn't trying to impress anyone—and a blouse on top.

"What are you here for?" asked Daniel suddenly. "Sorry, I didn't mean it to come out like that, but I wasn't really expecting you. Is there anything . . .?"

"I just wanted to see if there were any knickknacks of Alan's."

"Well, I haven't really touched his office. I've taken some files away, but most of it's still intact in there."

"Good," I said. "You don't mind if I go in and . . .?"

"Well, it's unusual," said Daniel, "but do you want me to accompany you?"

"Probably best not, Daniel," I said. "I could be a little on the tearful side. I'd rather have time on my own. I want to sit where he sat. I want to feel the last remnants of him."

My eyes started to well up, but in truth, I wasn't sad. I wasn't in a state of remorseful remembrance. Inside, I was almost jumping like an excited school child, but on the outside, tears were flowing. You don't do amateur drama for twenty years without some sort of ability. I'll have you know, I played Lady Macbeth and a few other of the classics and some modern stuff.

That's the thing about drama. It teaches you a lot of things. I also played a mermaid once and, well, I think that was about as close as anyone got in our little theater to having a severe lack of clothing. There was nothing rude or that, but to have the guts to stand up there, all the lights on, people looking at me, and probably a lot more of my body on show than I realized, especially around the midriff.

People always talk about the top half, but that's not where the weight comes on, is it? It's on the hips. It's on the belly. That's the funny side, though. Alan said to me afterwards when I mentioned I thought my tummy might have looked big, sticking out over the fish gill-decorated tights, "Who was looking at your belly?" Then he suddenly caught himself for what he'd said.

I knew what the implication was. So did he. And that's what I mean. It taught me to stand out in front of people, whatever my situation, however I am, and act normally or act in character, and not be afraid of what they're seeing.

I walked into the office, tears streaming down my face, and Daniel was upset for me. Inside, I wailed for about five minutes. Daniel came in to see if I was all right. When he told me I sounded like I was in distress, I said to him, "Could I have half an hour, twenty minutes? Would you mind disappearing off to get some coffee or tea and bring it back?"

It almost feels bad to play on people's good nature in that way, but it had to be done. He was only out the door when I turned and started going through the files. I used my phone to photograph as many as possible, picking out all the addresses, making sure Randazzo was involved. Randazzo was just about Alan's only client because it was so involved and Randazzo wanted to control him. He didn't want him to have other clients.

So, Alan was paid very well by him to look after his affairs wholly, apart from a few legacy clients. Well, legitimate affairs. Daniel took half an hour, and I think part of that was him just staying out of the way. When he came back in, my eyes were red, and I told him I was feeling much better. In the old days, before mobile phones, I'd have had a camera. I remember one of those little spy ones that Kelly used to have. It was inside a pen or something ridiculous like that. But I walked out with my phone loaded with information.

I went home that night and sat looking through all the addresses. I couldn't believe the number of businesses that Randazzo was involved in. If I attacked him, however I was going to do it, I wondered how long it would take him to understand that he was being attacked. The enormity of the task was dawning on me. This was going to be a long haul, if I was going to bring his organization down, if I was going to make them all pay in whatever way.

I've never been a great person for flowers, and when I saw Orchard Hill Flowers in one photograph, it just seemed natural. A very soft target as well. Who attacks a florist? Although it wasn't a florist, it was the warehouse. He controlled most of the flowers that came into the city; even independent florists probably got most of their stock from him.

Randazzo was a heck of an operator. Along with the warehouse, however, there was a chain, albeit small, of florists ran by Randazzo. The largest of them was just around the corner from a nightclub Randazzo owned. In fact, they had several properties and different business interests in that area, and I wondered if it was a hub. Was he based in there too?

I hadn't gained a gun at that point, and I needed to get one, but it couldn't be registered. I didn't think this would be that difficult, but I'd have to leave it for another time. I wanted to get started, for I was like a giddy schoolgirl. However, the next morning, I went to the gym with Patsy, and then I spent the next three days watching the florists.

I watched their daily routine. I saw they shut up at five, and I saw the gas station down the road. It occurred to me that the station got a delivery of gas late at night, just after eleven. That's when I got the idea. I would jump whoever was in that gas tanker. I would drive it at the shop and jump out. There would be an enormous crash, an explosion, a fire!

I would then run off, leaving a little memento, a miniature bottle of hooch, potcheen, whatever you wanted to call it. I made labels, small ones with the words 'Jac Moonshine' on them. I was coming into character.

I spent a morning standing in front of the mirror dressing in blacks, reds, yellows, looking at how to mask my face, and ended up with what I could only describe as a Dick Turpin-esque, a bandana covering from my nose down. On top of my head, I wore a black fedora. A fedora stood for women's rights and liberation and assertiveness. The rest of the costume was black except for a scarlet band. Well, I needed a bit of class, didn't I?

I got a handgun. It was the most bizarre thing. Eddie Tumbler came round a little drunk, and I had to take some overzealous action from him. Don't get me wrong, I didn't go to bed with him or anything. Because of the mood he was in, and because I wanted him to feel that he was protecting me and I was buying into it, I asked if I could have a gun. He dropped it round the next day, sat there showing me how to operate it. I even picked up a few mistakes in what he said. I also thought it was ironic that I might use this on him one day.

It was a day later when I was sitting at eleven o'clock in some bushes not far away from the gas station. The roads were quiet, having calmed down two or three hours beforehand, and I watched as the driver pulled up in his tanker and got out to talk to the attendant. It was the usual thing they did. After all, he had to hook up the pipes, and then put the gas into the underground storage. By the time he'd reached the main building beyond the forecourt, I was in the cab, and I was off. The keys had been left in, and it was so easy.

I wasn't the greatest driver of a tanker, but I got it rolling. I took it around two corners, built the speed up, and aimed it. Though it was only going around thirty miles an hour, maybe even less when I opened the cab door and jumped out, the tanker drove straight into the shop front.

In some ways, it was disappointing. Yes, there was the crash of the glass pane shattering as the truck barreled in. It was stopped a quarter in, three quarters out, but the tank had punctured. The gasoline poured out across the shop front. I stood quite a distance away, took out my gun, and held it steady.

"Remember to breathe," Jorge said in my head. "Detach

yourself from what you are doing."

I fired a couple of shots. Gasoline ignited. The building burned, and I turned to run away, but a shot whistled past my head. It had come from not that far away, and I saw a security guard.

Where had he come from? From which building? He hadn't been there on the previous nights.

I acted instinctively, fired my gun, and watched him go down. Until that point, there was no fear. Until that point, I was fine, but now my heart thumped. Was he all right?

I ran over to him, kicked the gun he'd dropped away, and stared down, still in my mask and fedora. The pain on his face was horrible. Then I heard sirens, and I ran down several streets until I got to where my car was parked. I opened the trunk, flung in my fedora, my mask, took off the jacket I was wearing, jumped into the front of the car, and drove far away from what I'd just done.

By the time I got home, Kelly was already in bed. I sneaked up into my room and changed into my pajamas and dressing gown before she saw anything of me. I went downstairs and sat watching the news. There was live footage of the fire. It had consumed two buildings, not just the one. Oh, the flower shop was destroyed, but who knew about the one beside it? The security guard was in hospital, status unknown. That's when I stood up and ran to the bathroom, and I vomited. Not once, but several times. Turmoil set in: had I killed an innocent man?

Chapter 06

The next day, I did nothing. Just sat huddled up on the sofa. I was a mess. My hair, which always looked tidy, was in lumps, knots, and all over the place. Kelly asked me if I was all right and if she could get me anything. I really must have looked bad, because Kelly rarely looks beyond herself.

I sat shaking almost in a cold sweat, especially when they reported about the guard's health. I mean, he'd shot at me. What was I to do? Then there were people from the area asking, "How could this happen in what was a pleasant part of the neighborhood?"

It was a nice place. That was the thing. I was attacking Randazzo's legitimate operation. He operated them in wholesome places. That was the whole point. It was meant to look like a normal business enterprise, and here was I charging in like anything but normal. I cursed Randazzo several times for what I'd become. This hard-nosed woman, this woman who had planned this over the previous days, was struggling in an instant. Her character had fallen. Debbie was back.

When Patsy heard I wasn't well, she came round, sat with me, and talked endlessly. In fairness, it took my mind away from the television.

I hate rolling news. It just sits there, goading you to watch. I know what you're saying. Switch the TV off. If your TV isn't on, you can't see it. True, but you still know it's there. I needed to know if this guard was going to be all right. I needed to know, and so I sat there, images of the fire blazing through the night. Then Kelly came down, sat beside me, and watched the news.

"I mean, you've got to be a complete asshole to be doing that."

"Language," I said. It's an automatic response. I felt like I'd been saying language to the child for the last three years. I think it's when they move up schools, isn't it? Suddenly the vocabulary develops, or rather recedes, recedes back to words that mean nothing, words that sound loud and proud but say so very little.

Kelly didn't even make me a cup of coffee. That wasn't so bad, because Patsy had made sure I was well watered. I took a shower at one point, and it reminded me of playing Lady Macbeth, cleaning out the spot, trying to make myself clean again.

It was that afternoon when the news came through that the security guard would be paralyzed. The man would be in a wheelchair for the rest of his life, and I'd done that. I had condemned him.

I had a bath after that, and when I got out, I simply put on my dressing gown because I was going to pop downstairs, maybe grab a bottle of wine, and go to bed. Try to sleep off the way I felt.

I'd been sick again during the day. It wasn't from food poisoning. It wasn't from anything except the fear and the utter vileness I felt for myself. The doorbell rang as I was in the kitchen, and I answered it in my dressing gown.

Outside was Detective Frogg. I remembered him, and he asked to come in, saying he needed to ask me some questions. I sat on the sofa, legs hauled up and tucked in beneath me. I didn't make any effort to look good for the man. I didn't try to look like I was in any sort of normal state.

"Are you unwell?" he asked.

"I'm just not coping."

"You may find this an unusual question," said Frogg, standing up, "but has anyone offered to carry out any retribution for what happened to your husband? He worked for some nasty people, and from what I can gather, some nasty people sorted him out. I was just wondering if anyone offered to carry out a little revenge for you."

My heart was thumping. The attack had been seen as revenge, so were people looking at me? He wasn't, was he? He was asking if anybody had come to me, offered to do a job for me.

"You think somebody's trying to get back at who?" I asked. "That's a flower shop that went up last night. You are talking about that, aren't you?"

"Yes," said Frogg. "That flower shop is owned by Mr. Randazzo."

"I didn't know," I said. "Why would someone have a go at Randazzo for what happened to my husband?"

"You must know he had somebody sort him. You know your husband made a mistake. He insulted a friend of Mr. Randazzo."

"Randazzo killed him?" I blurted. "Why?"

"You've been kept out of a lot in this world," said Frogg. "I see that your husband probably had two worlds on the go and kept you from the rather nasty one. Probably wise of him. Please, if anyone comes to talk to you about carrying out revenge, do nothing yourself, and please, get in contact with me. The city doesn't want a bloodbath going on. I think someone's taking it into their head to do something about Mr. Randazzo. That person would be very brave, but extremely foolish. They'd also need to have a lot of friends. Either way, the city doesn't want this sort of thing on the streets. If I can be candid, if Randazzo and the other goons want to shoot themselves, big deal, but when other people get injured . . ."

My stomach churned, and I wanted to throw up again, but the years, all twenty of them, of acting in countless poorly watched productions, let me stay focused. My outside persona showed the tears of a grieving widow. Nothing more, nothing less. My protestations of having had nobody come to visit except for the likes of Randazzo and his people seemed to fall on Frogg's ears and gain an acceptance. It wasn't that difficult to play; after all, it was true. That's all who had visited apart from Patsy, and let's face it, Patsy would never be up for a revenge plot. Neither was Debbie, though. I thought Jac Moonshine might have been, but Jac Moonshine was struggling to come to the fore.

Frogg disappeared, and it was maybe three minutes later because the kettle had just boiled when my door was rapped again. When I opened it, Randazzo stood there. Unlike Frogg, who was very polite and had taken no interest in my appearance except to ask if I was okay, Randazzo took a long look at me standing in my dressing gown. He didn't ask to come in but stepped in and said he would have a coffee.

I knew how to play this game. I had to make sure he wasn't offended because if he was, he'd get nasty, so I asked instead did he want anything stronger? He said whiskey, and when I turned to walk to the kitchen, he landed an almighty smack on my backside. He was carrying a bag in his left hand, but the right hand landed the blow and stayed there. I felt the stirrings of anger in my core. Jac Moonshine, who had run away after the previous night, lifted her head.

"I have a bit of bad news," he said. "One of my florist shops got attacked. Did anybody come here asking for Alan or what happened to him, or anyone say to you they were interested in doing something for him?"

"How do you mean?" I asked softly.

"Some people get the idea that Alan was taken out for saying something wrong. Some people might think they can correct an issue that didn't happen."

"No one's been to me," I said. I poured the man his whiskey.

"Good," he said. He placed the bag up on the kitchen workbench and then came over, putting his arm around me. "I do like that gown," he said, "Certainly hugs that figure of yours." His hand went down the side of my arm and back again onto my bottom. "Can't be easy for you," said Randazzo, "it really can't. Need somebody to look after you. Here."

He reached suddenly inside the coat he was wearing and placed a check for ten thousand dollars on the counter. "There'll be more of those," he said. "All you've got to do is to be a good little girl. Don't talk to the police because they'll come hunting for you. They'll come sniffing around because they'll think something's up with what happened to Alan. You just get on with the rest of your life, and I'll be around to look after you. You'll like that, wouldn't you?"

The dressing gown was being pulled up behind me, and I could feel the air on my backside. I wanted to slap him. But

I didn't. What I wanted to do was grab his hair and nut him. I wanted to drive that nose up into his face, smash it through into the brain. I wanted to rip the man apart, but I didn't. Instead, I stood there and let him pass his hand over my bare backside. I turned, looked at the cheque, then reached up and kissed him on the cheek. He grabbed the back of my head and kissed me roughly instead, driving his lips into mine. I acquiesced, letting him enjoy his moment. He needed to see Debbie, roll-over Debbie, good little wife of Alan. I needed to be a good little whore for Randazzo. But Jac Moonshine was standing up inside me.

He broke off, taking his whiskey, and sat down on my sofa. "Have a look inside the bag," he said.

I opened it up and inside was a blouse, but it was sheer. It was quality silk, but it needed an undergarment if I put it on.

"Do you like it?" he said. "You've got a figure for it. I always said to Alan you had a figure. I don't know how you keep beating the rest of them off. You are the sort that I like. Good little woman. Does everything she needs to do, and I think you used to keep Alan happy. When you used to come to the weddings, always wearing that slightly daring stuff. I bet Alan never made you wear something as daring as that. Put it on for me. Come round the front here and put it on for me."

I picked up the bag and walked around in front of the sofa. Inside, I was shaking. Inside, I was angry too. If I had the gun on me, I'd have blown the man's head off, but part of me was telling myself, *Time to act. Time to wheedle my way into this man's world. From there, I'll rip it apart*. I remembered my acting, pretended I was on a stage as I let the gown drop and then put on the blouse in front of him.

"How would you like to come to a few shows with me?

Maybe the old nightclub. I've got some events coming up that I think you'd enjoy."

His eyes were swinging all over me, but inside of me, Jac Moonshine was whispering in my ear, telling me to make this stand for what was to come ahead. I only knew the legitimate side of his business. If I could get close to him, I might know the other sides. I might be able to act against them. I walked forward, bent over, and kissed him on the cheek before then kissing him on the lips. His hands roamed before he stood up, saying he had to go for he had something to take care of. He had me walk him to the door, say goodbye to him at the door wearing that shirt.

As he left, I closed the door. I took off the shirt and I threw it on the ground. I almost ripped it in half, but Jac inside stopped me. I needed it; I needed it intact. This was all just part of the game, part of hauling him in, part of making him putty in my hands. Respect would have to go out the window—decency, too.

I walked back into the living room, put on my dressing gown, and watched the television. The picture showed the flower shop on fire again but then cut to the wife of the guard whom I'd paralyzed. I got down on my knees in front of the television. "I'm sorry," I said out loud. "I'm sorry, but some people are going to get hurt," I said. "I'll try not to because a lot of other people who deserve it are going to get hurt a lot worse."

Chapter 07

Now, I don't want you getting the wrong idea about me. I would not sell my body just to find out what Randazzo was going to do. My plan wasn't to get into bed with him and pick up on the pillow talk to find out where I could damage his business. There was no way that man was going to get into bed with me. When something like this happens to you, there's so much that you can do differently than you did before, but there is a point.

What Alan and I had was sacred. Now, if in the future someone comes along who is as much to me as Alan was, fine. Perfectly normal, but I will not give my body up to someone just so I can exact revenge on him. With that in mind, I knew I'd have to do more than simply have Randazzo coming around for two reasons. I'd need to put the cold shoulder on him if I thought he was going to jump into bed with me, which might kill the flow of any information. Also, I needed to clarify what he was telling me.

When I was there as Debbie, he could have told me anything. He could just be soft soaping me. He wouldn't necessarily tell me what he was really thinking. To do that, I'd need to either find him alone, in his place of work or discussing with those closest to him. With that in mind, I tailed him one day after he called round.

Thankfully, I was in a decent state of dress and not in my dressing gown. He didn't stay too long, simply putting down another check for me, and having his usual exploration of my backside. When I saw him on the mobile in his car, I slipped on a wig, quickly did some makeup, and got into the car to see him driving off to the end of our road.

I tailed him, keeping as far back as possible in my station wagon before I saw him joined by another couple of men. Randazzo got out from behind the wheel into the passenger seat. This was clearly his heavy mob. It was quite something that he popped around to me without them, but then again, Debbie was no threat.

When he stopped and entered a restaurant on the better side of the city, I parked up and sat in a coffee shop across the road. For all I knew, he may even have owned that, but what I saw was he spent most of his day in that restaurant. Two days later, I popped into the restaurant on Saturday for a meal.

This time, I was young. I had blonde hair and was heavily made up with a fake tan. There are benefits to not working, having money paid to me, and that the day is my own. Kelly was back at college, but that suited me fine, for there were no awkward questions during the day about what I was going to do.

As I ate, I noted several waitresses. If I had to take a random distribution of waitresses in the city and ask, *What would the average waitress look like?* and then pick five waitresses to say this is the selection you would get, this restaurant would not have fitted those criteria. Mamma Pico's, as the restaurant was called, had an unusually good-looking selection of waitressing staff.

Over several visits, I also noted that Randazzo, when there, had an eye for women, not an appreciative one either, but a hungry one. I don't know if that was the way business ran amongst these people. Eddie Tumbler, when he was in, wasn't shy about looking either.

Alan would never have done that. I know because I once talked to him about it. If he saw someone he liked, he was very subtle about it. Casual glances when she wasn't looking or just looked the other way, certainly not allowing me to see. I had told him once, "It's fine, as long as that's all it is, that initial involuntary glance."

I always felt secure with Alan, not because he couldn't run off, not because he didn't have a choice, and not because he couldn't impress and win over another woman, but because he didn't want to. Before, I said that he owned me and I owned him. That's what made this so hard. Somebody took away what I owned.

At the end of my meal, I approached the maître d' and asked if there were any jobs going. They took me in front of Randazzo, who gave a quick nod after glancing at me up and down. It's testimony to the makeup abilities that I have that he didn't recognize me. Although, in fairness, I had on the drama group's rather large, padded bra. I wasn't quite the same shape as I normally was.

Over the coming weeks, I was able to take several shifts for Randazzo, who was talking to various of his chiefs. They talked in a code, but the code got less and less the longer I was there. I passed on nothing. I acted on nothing. Although I was still out condemning certain legitimate operations of his to a fiery end, I approached nothing that was on the illegal side.

I heard a few things. I heard about several people being removed from the operation. I heard the occasional instruction to lay it on heavy to people, and to remind people rather abruptly where their loyalties lay. There were words about drug shipments as well, but all quietly done.

My big break came when Randazzo was talking to Eddie Tumbler. I was in the far corner with the hoover going, and he must have believed that I couldn't hear them. Then, he raised his voice slightly because what I was doing must have been affecting their conversation. I heard the name Kozlov, and Columbia. Then, slapped down in front of Randazzo, was a picture of someone arriving at the airport. Eddie then talked more loudly, but Randazzo held up his hand, turned around to me, and motioned that I should cut the power. I did so.

They asked me to skedaddle for a bit. This wasn't uncommon. If they were going to talk about something very important, I was told to go into the back room. I left, but glanced down at the photograph. There was a man with a rather camp mustache. He was bald, and I tried to memorize the face. After spending five minutes in the back room doing nothing, the door opened, and Eddie Tumbler told me to come back in. As he did so, he then leaned back over his shoulder and said, "Friday night." Tumbler was told to have a waiting party.

I finished up my shift, went out to my car, sat down with my notebook, and wrote everything I'd heard about someone coming in from Columbia. I drew a picture of the man's photograph, especially the mustache.

There'd be a Friday night reception committee. He must have been bringing drugs or something else of note in. I checked my schedule for working at the restaurant and I wasn't on Friday night. I'd only had to do the very occasional night shift, and when I did that, I told Kelly I was off out at the gym or somewhere else. In truth, she didn't really care.

I think looking back through all of this, that's something that's bothered me. I never took care of Kelly, but I'll come to that. You don't realize what they can get up to.

I spent Friday evening waiting for the flight coming in from Columbia. When it touched down, I sat and watched various men and women exiting the arrivals lounge. There was an arrivals committee waiting for this man and I wondered just where they would meet to exchange drugs inside an airport. That would be far too risky, wouldn't it?

If the man arrived and got caught at the airport, Randazzo wouldn't want his people to be about. They would meet somewhere outside the airport. I decided I needed to intercept the man before he left the terminal. The joy of Mannersberg is although it has an international airport, there aren't that many flights, and the one from Columbia came only twice a week.

I was sitting with a long coat on which I had tailored. It sat well on my shoulders, but inside there was a significant amount of room because the coat widened out. Sitting down and watching the arrivals, I saw a face I recognized from the photograph on the table at the restaurant. I stood up, walking slowly until I was within reasonable distance of the man.

I saw him look over towards the men's toilets and then he almost half shook his head and walked on again. He stopped for a moment, looking at a sign above, and then he headed off in another direction. He wasn't heading for the exit, somewhere else instead. I saw him take a walk towards an accessible toilet. It was set back from the main concourse. I'm not sure how much it was used.

I saw him turn a corner and ran to get close. As I turned the corner, he'd already opened the door of the disabled toilet and was stepping inside. I was blocked from his view being on the other side of the door, so I quickly grabbed the handle as he went to close it from the other side. When I spun around the corner of the door, he looked surprised, but not as surprised as when the left jab he got to the face arrived. I then kicked him hard on the knee. He folded forward and received my knee in his face.

I closed the door quickly behind me as he lay sprawled inside. I had to pull his legs hard to make sure the door closed. I locked it. I put a hand inside the pocket of my coat and forced the fabric forward so it looked like I was holding a weapon inside my pocket.

"Randazzo wants his goods," I said.

"Randazzo? I'm meant to meet his people," said the man in rather broken English.

"Yes, but change of plan. I will take it to Randazzo."

"Did you have to be so rough?" asked the man. "We had a place to meet."

"The place was compromised. Where is the merchandise?"

I did not know what the man was bringing in, other than it was drugs. He hauled himself off the floor and sat down on the toilet seat. He lifted the briefcase he had with him, popped it open, then took two keys out from two separate pockets. He opened a lock that was hidden underneath part of the briefcase, then he rolled back another bit of the sidewall and clicked a lock there. A thin layer inside the briefcase slid out.

I wasn't sure how many drugs were there. In fact, I had no idea what a significant amount of drugs even looked like. I'd never taken them in my life. Surely there must be some drugs that, in certain quantities, are worth a bit, while the same quantity of another drug is worth a lot more. Either way, it must be significant, and it was incredibly clever how the man had got the drug through customs to march in boldly with a briefcase full of it.

I didn't want to look like an amateur, though, so I didn't ask how. I just looked at what had been slid out. There were two packets, both very thin. I reached down for them both.

"No," said the man. "That one is yours on the left. The one on the right is for Donovan."

I looked at the man with indignation. "Donovan? Mr. Randazzo does not like that. Randazzo runs this town. You only deal with Randazzo."

"Kozlov said it's fine. Kozlov said I could come with this. I meant no disrespect."

I smacked him across the face with the back of my left hand but still keeping the right hand inside my jacket. Of course, I didn't have a gun with me. I wasn't going to walk into an airport with a gun. How do you explain that one away? I always thought airports would be difficult to get out of in a hurry because they have security guards. Most of what I had done was at night and attacking soft targets, those with little security.

"Mr. Randazzo is not happy about two players. Tell Mr. Kozlov he's to come here and discuss the entire operation. He comes, and we end up with one buyer, just Mr. Randazzo. He'll take care of Mr. Donovan for you."

I picked up the packets, putting them into the interior pocket of my coat. For a moment, my hand came away out of the right-hand pocket and the pretense of a gun being in there was shattered. The man opposite me, sitting on the toilet, was not daft. As soon as he saw that, he reached for me. He grabbed my arm, and he threw a punch that caught me on the shoulder.

It was weak. I had fought with better in the gym over these last fifteen years. I elbowed him in the face three times. He was out cold, blood running down from his nose. I finished packing the drugs away inside my jacket pocket, then took out a small bottle of hooch with the label Jac Moonshine on it and placed it inside the man's jacket. I undid the lock, opened the door, and shut it behind me.

I then tried to walk as naturally as possible out to the car park where my car was sitting. Before I reached it, I popped into the ladies' toilets, took off the jacket, unfolded it, removed the blonde-haired wig I was wearing. I didn't have time to take off the makeup I was in, but I'd seen where the cameras were in the car park, and I kept my back to them once I had got out to the car.

You might wonder what I did with the drugs. Well, there's only one place for those. I stopped on the bridge, going over the Sunnyside river just outside the city. I cut a hole in each packet, and I let the merchandise dissolve into the water. I do not know if it's bad for the wildlife, but those drugs would not do any harm to any kids.

The next day Randazzo came round to my house. He was livid. He sat on my sofa as I sat beside him in my dressing gown, slowly stroking the back of his neck. He sat and told me something had gone wrong. He raged that someone had left him a bottle, someone called Jac Moonshine.

I'll not lie to you. The excitement of playing this part of the ignorant and submissive Debbie while all the time Jac Moonshine sat opposite him, controlling him, playing with his organization and his mind, brought me a great joy. Power is one thing, but the ability to get in and mess with someone's mind, to twist them from the inside out, it's a drug, but it's a dangerous one. Possibly more dangerous than the ones that flew in from Columbia that night.

Chapter 08

A small bottle of hooch labeled with *Jac Moonshine.* I said earlier I'd tell you where that came from. Now's about as good a time as any.

I grew up in Ireland, on a farm out on the west coast. My father never wanted me to run that farm because he hated running it. He did, however, like making potcheen, or moonshine, as some call it. Illicit alcohol has got so many names, and if I'm honest, I can't stand the stuff. Maybe I've just got a more refined taste these days. I like a glass of wine, something dark, fruity.

Back then, we used to grow a lot of potatoes on the farm and my father would grate some of them and make potcheen. It was, of course, illegal, but the best thing about being out there on the west of Ireland wasn't simply the view out to the Atlantic where you would stand and see the weather rolling in, bank upon bank of rolling cloud gradually approaching the shore until it dumped on you. Now, the second-best thing about living out there was that people had an understanding about letting go of those things that are technically illegal but which work for everyone. Potcheen was one of those things.

My father used to hide it in a small building at the far end of our farm. I remember going down with him when I was young, helping him carry the crates of it, and we stacked them up and he made me count them. I think there were over three hundred bottles there. I had cleaned all the bottles for him and rinsed them out.

The bottles had all sorts of labels on them, for he'd got them from the pub down the road, which he frequented. They would have whiskey bottles that were being thrown out, kept round the back and which, mysteriously, weren't taken away by the bin men. They were taken away by my father to the building on the edge of our farm.

Several days, I'd take a wheelbarrow and go back and forth, probably about half a mile to the site of his still. He was supervising the making of the potcheen, but I came with bottles cleaned down at the old building because it had a running tap. My father would fill the bottles up and then I'd take them down in the wheelbarrow.

However, each time I'd take a third of the number of bottles down that I'd brought up because of the weight of the potcheen inside. We'd counted three hundred that time, and my father took me down the next week and asked me to count the bottles again. There were two hundred and seventy. My father reckoned that was about six bottles per police officer in the local area.

When they said local area, that was reasonably extensive. The local Garda constable would take them, dole them out, and it made sure that nobody came to annoy my father. As illicit booze, he didn't sell it. That was a key factor. He wasn't making money out of it, but my father's booze ended up in every house in the district except for one. The only man that ever complained about him was Dermot Marlow.

He was an incomer, as they delicately put it, a teetotaler, and he would stand in the village with pamphlets telling everyone that God was coming. I have nothing against anyone who wants to stand there. I went to church for most of my life. Catholic when I was in Ireland, a Protestant one here in the States, and I'm quite with it. Treat your neighbor right. Look after each other. Somebody must have made us. I don't see why it couldn't have been God, but Dermot was determined that whatever happened, my father's potcheen should not be tolerated.

I remember him coming into the bar. I was only fourteen sitting at the back because the licensing laws didn't really apply out there. Not that they were handing out drinks to anyone who was underage. There was cola, but that was fine because the music was playing. Everybody was having fun. There was a line of dark stout running down the bar, each one at a different point of settling.

A small crowd of us teenagers were occasionally sent up to fetch drinks for the adults, but were otherwise sitting and laughing in the corner, listening to the music and occasionally playing it. It wasn't my forte, but the others did. I could get up and do some Irish dancing when called upon.

Dermot marched in telling everyone that they were all damned, had a go at the owner of the bar, a James McLaughlin, a giant of a man, telling him he was being outdone by my father's potcheen. James told him he made plenty of money from the people in here. In fact, he took a bottle from behind the bar. It said it was whiskey, but the color was wrong. He poured a rather stout tumbler and downed it in front of Dermot.

"There," he said. "Excellent stuff, excellent." He turned and toasted my father. I remembered summers, going back and forward with the bottles, sitting behind my father at the still, running out to him with the wheaten bread from my mother, massive slabs of butter on it, and a cup of tea that was almost as thick as molasses. They were good times. I had a heck of an upbringing. We didn't have everything, but I learned about family.

My mother and father were an odd couple in some ways, but she ran the house. He ran everything outside of the house. He never questioned her about any decision in the house, and she never questioned him. I remember the day there was trouble, though.

A couple of youths had decided they were going to break windows. They were seen as a bad lot by the villagers, which probably didn't help, but they came up to my father with a knife, threatening to take away anything he had, including his beloved potcheen, unless he gave them money. My father was not a violent man. He would walk away from a fight, though he would tell you what was right and wrong. His moral compass wasn't perfect, but it set me up reasonably well.

I remember these kids at the door, punks sixteen, seventeen, eighteen maybe. I was twelve, hiding behind him, watching as they pulled a flick knife out on him. My mother came to the door, pushed me behind her, stood beside my father.

"You'll give them no money. No money, Michael," she said to him. The one with the knife lunged at my father. My mother pushed him out of the way, and she hit the guy with a rolling pin. I always thought they were used for baking, but my mother could use it as an offensive weapon.

Another punk threw a punch that caught my mother on the shoulder. But my father lost it, for the first time in my life, and I saw my father drive into him with his shoulder. He put the punk on the floor, stood over him, and hit him repeatedly. My mother beat the head off the other two before pulling my father back off the other one. The teenagers were battered.

I was always amazed at my mother stepping forward to support my Da. They were a unit, you see. Whatever was his role, whatever he had to do, however they defined it, she would support him in it and vice versa. She told me they owned each other. I remember asking her what that meant, and she turned to me and said, "This," her hands running down the front of her body, indicating all of it. "Your father owns this, and I own all of him. When he hurts, I hurt. When he must fight, I fight. When he cries, I cry with him. Everything he is, I am. And he, me."

I guess that's where I learned what it was to be a partner. I won't say wife because the role I fulfilled in some ways was different. I did things that my mother didn't do. There were parts of looking after the family finances that got left to me because Alan said I needed to learn that side of things in case he ever went bad. Alan took on a lot with Kelly because he wanted to. Alan cooked about forty percent of the time. He liked it and enjoyed it. I cooked the other sixty because I was home. We may have divided the jobs up differently, but I learned we were each other. We owned each other.

One summer, an Irish soldier arrived in the community. He was upstanding, an absolute gem of a man and around about my mother and father's age. She blew him away. Truly, he loved her, and he struggled when she invited them round to the house because my father was there, and he would see them holding hands.

I asked her when I was older, was she ever tempted by him?

She told me yes. She told me she would've struggled if he had made his way further into her life. She said that one evening after my father had fallen asleep, she stood at the door with this broad-shouldered, gorgeous man, and she said they almost kissed, but he put a hand up in front of her lips and he said to her, you don't break into a partnership like she had. That was wrong. If he did it, he would deserve every bit of hellfire the priest could rain on him.

He said he'd seen action and he'd killed men, who then left wives behind. He'd broken relationships. He'd broken marriages through what he had to do in the war. He said that the church talked about ultimate sins, and he felt he had committed them in doing this to men and women. He said he would do it no more and turned and walked out of my mother's life.

She thanked him. She said that to me. She thanked him. She even sent him scones and wheaten bread, for he continued to live in the village for a while. Apparently, he married five years later. My mother and father attended the wedding, toasting him, cheering him and his bride. It stuck with me.

You don't do that. It's the ultimate sin. Randazzo committed the ultimate sin against me. That's why there was retribution. That's why he had to face hell. The other bit came from Jorge. Jorge said to me I had to scare him. Not just harm him, but get inside his head.

I remembered the potcheen. Several years ago, my father brought a few bottles over. I poured them into smaller ones, ready to give them out to the family in small doses as Christmas presents over the following years. Then Alan was killed. I didn't want to give them to anybody then. I wanted to use them.

Randazzo wouldn't understand why. He wouldn't understand that potcheen represented the fact that we should do good to everyone. There's a standard at which you interact with your community. It's not about law and order. It's about doing what's right. You may look at me and think that there's something askew, that I'm wrong in the acts I carried out, the willful destruction, the fact I wanted to kill the man. The fact I wanted to kill not just him, but I was quite happy to take out any of the other evil sods that wanted to work with him. You may think there's a darkness in me.

Well, I have news for you. There's a darkness in all of us, and it's there to be used. It's there for times such as this. It's there for times when retribution must be shared. No one will step in for me. Alan was a good man who just got on the wrong side of someone, who said the wrong word or pass a smile. By rights, the law should find out who killed him, but they won't.

We have to change our society; we have to sort it. We must take steps ourselves. I wouldn't remain a good little housewife. I wasn't brought up that way. I was brought up to stand with my man, and if he was attacked, I would defend him. Now he's been killed. I would avenge him, and by dropping a little potcheen, a bit of hooch, I would scare Randazzo. He broke up something that should never be broken. He committed the ultimate sin.

Randazzo and Kozlov had to pay for that because nobody else would step in and save me. Nobody else would stop them from coming around. It started with me, and they tried to turn me into one of their women, the ones beyond their wives that they used and played with. Then it would be Kelly. God help me if they touched Kelly. I would kill them right where they stood. Alan would've done the same. But instead of rolling over and just letting them do what they wanted with me, I stood with my husband. I would destroy them. In doing so, I would honor my mother and father with a bit of hooch, a little of homespun alcohol that said just where this revenge was coming from.

Chapter 09

I could say that when I started out on this trip that I wasn't fully aware of how serious it was, but that would be wrong. I was fully aware of how serious. I just didn't get how horrific things could come.

I decided I would teach Kelly how to defend herself because I couldn't be sure I would always be there. The one thing I didn't want to do was let Kelly be complicit in the advances of anyone like Randazzo or Eddie Tumbler. I've lived a life. I understand men, and to a degree, I can play them. Don't get me wrong. I don't want to. I never played Alan. Everything that exchanged between Alan and me was complementary. We worked off each other and he would never want to do anything that would upset or harm me, and me neither to him.

If I was having a day when I wasn't feeling good and Alan felt amorous, I just told him and he stopped and he asked me what was wrong and tried to help solve whatever that was. Not that he always could, but that wasn't his fault. What I'm saying is I couldn't see the likes of Randazzo or Eddie Tumbler stopping because I'm all akilter. The same with Kelly.

The problem I had with teaching Kelly to defend herself was I couldn't do it in the house. Oh, by the way, Kelly, we could have several mob figures after us. Why don't we do this instead? I told her we needed to stay close together and she could join me at one of the boxercise classes I took. She's only eighteen, so she doesn't have a lot of the muscle I have in my arms from having trained for so long, but she's spritely on her feet.

Kelly joined me. She kept up with me until the end of the class where we stood together, gulping down water like it was going out of fashion.

"Do you want to see what else I do at the gym?" I asked her.

"No," said Kelly. "I mean, this is all just aerobics, isn't it? They call it boxercise, but you're not really boxing."

"You think I can't hit something? You think I'm weeny because all I do is jump around in a form instead of actually tackling something? You come with me."

I didn't give her a choice but marched her into the gym where a bag was hanging at the far end. There was no one on it, and the gym was quiet, so I donned some gloves and began to tap it. Kelly stood beside me.

"You're not really hitting that though, are you?" she said.

I showed her what I could do. I lashed out with my legs left and right, followed up with combination punches. You didn't do mixed martial arts the time I'd done them without learning a bit. Don't get me wrong. I will not be the next leader of the Shaolin Temple, but I can handle myself.

I could tell Kelly was impressed because I didn't just kick the bag for a couple of minutes. I kept going for the next five and then five more. By the time I'd finished, the sweat was dripping off me and I reached for a water bottle before looking at her face. Kelly was proud, but in typical teenage fashion, she didn't tell me so. She simply said, "That wasn't bad."

"You next," I told her, and I could see her back away. "No," I said, "You next. You haven't got Dad anymore. We need to protect ourselves. You're getting to an age where a guy might try to, well, you know."

"What?" asked Kelly.

"Maybe force things a little."

"What makes you think that's going to happen?"

"You never know. Look, stand here and watch my hand." I showed her how to punch properly and then I showed her how to use the legs. "Punches first," I said. "Hit it." She threw a punch at the bag that I would've been embarrassed by.

"No, put your shoulder into it. Throw it, hit it. Hit it as if that bag's done something to you."

Kelly threw a punch and yes, it was better, but she wasn't channeling herself into it. I could change the form, but she needed to learn to fight from within.

"Hit it like it's the person who killed Da."

"That's not funny, Mom. That's not funny."

"I'm not being funny. Why do you think I hit so hard? Go on. Imagine who it is. Hit it like this." I thudded a fist into the bag.

She threw the next one harder, but I told her there was more in there, told her she could see him, told her she knew who did it and he was standing before her, told her to let loose. She whipped a leg up into the bag. The angle of attack was all wrong. She was off balance when she did it, not planting herself correctly, but the anger that came out through that leg, the channeled aggression, was excellent.

"Good," I said. "Now do it again." This time I caught her as she went to fall over.

"Thing is, you're doing well with channeling hate, the hatred, the anger, but you got to learn to have the right form as well." We spent the next half hour working on her form, and since Alan had died, it was about the closest we'd been. Towards the end, I noticed that someone was standing on the other side of the gym watching us. I cast a glance and saw it was Randazzo and he was making his way over.

I leaned into Kelly, "Say nothing unless asked," I said, "and don't mention that you've been hitting the person who killed Da; don't mention that at all unless you have to."

"Why?" asked Kelly.

"Randazzo's coming over. Just don't."

"Well, well, you're certainly a dark one, Debbie. Didn't know you could hit like that. I enjoy seeing a woman sweat."

He put his hand up to my cheek, ran it down onto my shoulder and down past my arm.

"You look good like that. Very good."

If you ever wanted to feel like a piece of meat, you just needed to meet this man. The eyes were everywhere, and the conversation was banal. He's no charmer. I've met charmers in my time. I know what they're looking for might be the same end product, but at least they have the decency of pretending it's some sort of competition. With Randazzo, you feel you're a joint of beef on the rack, waiting to be picked and put into the trolley for a Sunday lunch.

"It's just a bit of fun exercise," I said to him. "Just out with Kelly, maybe offer her a bit of protection."

"I'm all the protection you need," said Randazzo. "Told you that. I'll look after you. Can't be easy without a man around the house."

Inside, my blood was boiling. I wanted to show Kelly exactly how hard I could hit. I wanted to take the head off the man right there. Wasn't that the point of what I was teaching her, controlled aggression? I needed to be in a place where I could do that. I needed to make him feel pain. If I hit him here, his men would step in, and besides, I wasn't prepared to just simply take him out. He had to suffer.

Randazzo put his arm around me, pulling me close, but my primary concern was I saw some of his men behind Kelly. When I saw her jump, I nearly tore out of Randazzo's arms. I nearly went straight for the man behind her, but Randazzo could tell I'd moved.

"Good ass on this one, boss. Maybe double what you want."

"What?" raged Randazzo. "What do you mean?"

"Nothing, boss. I was just saying."

The man looked panicked, very panicked. He should have been; he was just lucky that I was being restrained by Randazzo. I felt his arms come away from me and he pushed Kelly out of the way, walking up to the man.

"You don't get to talk about my women like that. You don't get to talk like that at all."

Suddenly, he punched him once, twice, three times, and the man hit the floor. Randazzo then kicked him right in the gut. It didn't bother me. He had just grabbed our Kelly. Kelly was shocked having never seen such violence. I put my arms around her, turned her head away, but I watched as Randazzo's henchmen turned on one of their own when he instructed them to, and kicked him to pieces.

It lasted less than a minute, but by the time they walked away, the man was an utter mess. There was blood on the floor and on the walls. With a click of his fingers, Randazzo sent one of his men outside.

He turned back to me, putting an arm on my shoulder, and

then stepped across to give me a kiss on the cheek.

"You see, Debbie, I'll protect both of you. Look after the pair of you." His left hand reached over and started running through Kelly's hair. She looked up, crying. "I'm sorry, little one," he said. "Sorry you had to see that. Sorry that he did that to you. I'm here to protect you and your mom. A gorgeous looking girl like you doesn't need hands like that."

He was saying all this with his hand on me. I was well aware of where they'd been in the past. The other thing that bothered me was Eddie Tumbler was there. He'd put in a few good boots into the man on the floor, but his eyes were all at Kelly. Sometimes men like that know they've lost the battle. Randazzo was the boss, and Eddie Tumbler would have to take him out if he wanted me.

I wasn't worth that much to him because he didn't know my true value. Men like that don't. Alan did. Hopefully, Kelly would find someone else that would.

The way Eddie Tumbler looked at her that day, even my blood began to boil. You see, I said that I didn't know how hard this would be. Well, I didn't know how bloody it would be, and I thought I could do it without Kelly getting involved. But that day, that day was the first day that I saw her starting to be brought into this. She was eighteen. She should have had a couple of years at school, gone off to college somewhere or gone and toured Europe and had the time of her life. She would not have a grease ball like that staking a claim on her.

The doors of the gym opened, and it was then I noticed the few other people who were there. The weights had stopped. They were watching, half in terror of what Randazzo had done.

The sports center manager marched into the gym, saw Randazzo and came up before him, almost bowing his head.

"Would you like me to clean up?" he asked.

"My boys will deal with the main mess once they've lifted him out of the way."

"Of course, Mr. Randazzo. A terrible accident, but we'll have it cleaned up soon enough." The sports center manager turned around to the rest of the people in the gym. "Please, please, incident's over. Terrible accident and a terrible fall for the young man. We'll have this cleaned up in a jiffy. Please go back to your working out."

Randazzo stood watching his henchman pick up the mess of a man. He was barely walking and I'm sure his nose was busted; possibly a couple of ribs by the way he clutched at his innards.

"That's the trouble these days," said Randazzo. "People don't know their place. I hope you know your place, Kelly," he said, reaching out and putting a hand on her cheek. "Your mom knows her place. Don't you? His hand went down my back and very deliberately he grabbed my backside."

"I'm just thankful you were here. It's not easy without Alan. Difficult without someone to protect us." I reached up and gave Randazzo a kiss on the cheek. He turned instead, kissing me on the lips right in front of Kelly. "I'll be seeing you," he said to me. "You too, Kelly. Take care of your mom."

He walked off, stopping at the door and looked back at us, and then he was gone. Kelly fled into my arms.

"How, Mom? How do you do that? Why do you let him kiss you like that?"

"Then do what, Kelly? You saw the man on the floor. People like that, you've got to play. Time will come."

"How?" asked Kelly. "How's our time going to come against somebody like that? We should just get up and go."

"Not here, Kelly," I said. "Not in front of people with ears. People with ears talk and you don't know who to. Just trust your mom. I have it all under control and I need you to trust me." Kelly looked down at the mess on the floor and at the staff who had come in to clean it.

"Like he trusted Randazzo?"

The door of the gym opened again, and I saw Detective Frogg arriving. He marched over, looking at me curiously, then at Kelly, before staring at the floor, which was being cleaned.

"A lot of blood about," said Frogg. "What happened?"

"Somebody took a tumble, lost control," said the manager. "Unfortunate, really, but it's okay, all getting cleaned up. It's in the accident book if you want to look at it," he said to Frogg.

"If I wanted to read fiction, I'd go to the library." Frogg glanced over at me. "Are you two okay?"

"It was a bit of a shock," I said. "Kelly's a little put out by it. Never seen somebody have an accident like that before."

"Was the ambulance called?" Frogg asked.

"No," said the manager. "Some of his friends have taken him away. I'm sure they'll be taking him to a doctor. We're just making sure the mess is cleared up."

Frogg looked down again at the disappearing crime scene and looked over at me.

"If you need any help, you have my number," he said.

"We're fine," I said. "We're just fine."

Once he'd left the room, I went with Kelly to the showers, determined to put the incident behind us. As I stood washing my hair, Kelly was in the cubicle beside me. I could hear her sobs. I had every reason to want Randazzo dead. I had every reason to take out every one of those henchmen, but that day had given me more reason. Not only had they killed my man, but now they were looking to angle in on my daughter. They were looking to take over our lives.

I was no piece of meat on a shelf, and neither would Kelly be. One day, she'd have a man who respected her. She'd become one with him, lean on each other like Alan and I had. Until that day, not one of these bastards would lay his hands on her.

I washed myself down, listening to her occasional sobs, telling her across the showers that it would be all right and to trust her mom. What I didn't realize was it had pulled her in and I couldn't stop her from getting any deeper.

Chapter 10

I'd been leaving the little bottles of hooch and thinking I was making my mark. After all, the logo said on it, "Jac Moonshine." I thought it was obvious to someone like Randazzo that Jac Moonshine was attacking him, but it wasn't so, and I was quite indignant when I found out. I'd stopped working as a waitress at the restaurant that Randazzo frequented, and instead I started going to it as an elderly woman. I'd dress up in gray hair, pearl necklace, some rogue hair even appearing from the side of my cheek, the lines drawn on, and a croaky old voice.

I'd been several times, popping in announcing I enjoyed the food, and taking a table on my own. I always remember that night though, because as I was entering, Randazzo was coming in behind me. One of his henchmen went to push me to one side. I was arched over, faking I had a hunched back, and I heard Randazzo clip the guy around the back of the head. Then this hand appeared, taking my hand and offering to escort me inside. He placed me at a table and said I should have whatever I wanted; it was on the house. He then sat within my earshot, and for the next hour, I completely ignored him, or at least he thought so.

I ordered several types of food, sending half of it back uneaten. When he asked me what I was doing, I said I was trying everything like he'd offered. He seemed to find that quite funny, telling the man who was with him that old people knew how to make use of whatever they're given. He told me to keep at it, but as I sat there, he got a visit from Eddie Tumbler.

"We've picked him up, boss," said Tumbler, sitting down. They put a bowl of pasta in front of the man, and he ate with Randazzo.

"Who?" asked Randazzo.

"O'Rourke. We've picked him up."

"Good. Where's he being held?"

"The warehouse down on the docks. Got a few of them trying to get the location of the drugs out of him. He's hung upside down in there, turning him over. Won't be long before he spills something. You think he's working alone?"

"You mean O'Rourke? Possibly. Two-bit punk, been all over the soft targets, hasn't he? Gone after me in places I can't defend that well. All the legitimate businesses. And then there was the airport deal with the Columbian shipment. Not happy with that one, Eddie. He's forced me to get Kozlov back over. Kozlov's not keen about that either. I'm going to have to compensate him for those drugs if we don't find them.

"Donovan's kicked off, too. Been a few incidents over that as well. Kozlov wasn't happy, said I shouldn't be interfering in those deals, but even if O'Rourke's done this, he was right. Should have been coming to me. We'll get Kozlov over again, thrash it out, but I need to be seen to be dealing with this. Clearly Donovan can't."

Randazzo looked agitated, and clearly the Kozlov connection

was big to him. I didn't understand how much drug traffic flowed through that way, what type they were, but I knew that the man meant something to him. If Kozlov came over, I could take him out, kill off a supply line. I was quite taken by how public-spirited I was becoming, not just simply out for vengeance, but that was the principal goal. Destroy him. Destroy Randazzo.

"Do you want me to go back then—see what I get out of him?"

"No. You stay and eat with me. I've got some other things to discuss."

He put his hand up in the air and the waitress came over. When I'd worked there, this wasn't uncommon. He would tell you to get someone. Didn't tell you why. Just to do it. From the back room a few minutes later, a guy I recognized, Patrick, came out. I'd summoned him a few times when I'd been working there. Then Randazzo had him lean down and was whispering in his ear. I stood up, calling a girl in a croaky voice, asking for the bill, making sure Randazzo could hear. He finished talking to Patrick and then sent him over towards me.

"Hey grandma, I told you, there's no bill."

"What?" I said, putting my hand to my ear. "Bill who?"

"Don't pay," said Randazzo. "Patrick, help her out. She got a taxi or something?"

"Have you got a taxi, love?" asked Patrick in my ear.

"I got a car. What do I want a taxi for?"

I took a five-dollar bill out of my pocket and waved it over towards one waitress. She came and took it, and I felt Patrick take my arm. I made him wait at the curbside when he walked me out to my vehicle. Then I got into an old banger I had rented.

"Are you sure that car's going to get you home?" he asked.

"It's as fit as me, young man. Don't be cheeky."

I sat in the car, and he watched me drive off, but instead of going anywhere, I went around the block repeatedly until I saw Patrick get into a car of his own. I kept my distance but followed him down towards the docks, where I saw him pull into a vacant complex. As soon as he arrived outside of the building, a shuttered door was pulled up and he drove the car inside. I drove off and parked about four blocks away inside a car park. I sat in the car and wondered about what I'd heard. Eamon O'Rourke is what they'd said, getting the blame for the drug theft at the airport.

This wouldn't work, would it? Jorge had said I needed to make the man fear me, but he couldn't fear me if Eamon O'Rourke was the one getting done for this. Couldn't fear me if they thought they had him and were beating him up. I needed to be a ghost. I needed to be someone he didn't know, and I needed to set the record straight.

I got changed in the car as darkness fell, dressing up in my black trousers and top, the mask around my face, and the blonde hair hanging out of the back. Jac Moonshine was going to take to the street. I put a gun in my pocket.

I wrote a note with the words, "Who the hell is Eamon O Rourke?" and signed it, Jac Moonshine. I put that away in the pocket as well, and then walked from the car park round several blocks until the warehouse Patrick had driven into came into view.

I watched it from a distance and saw no one coming or going. There was only one entrance to the walled unit that had no windows, and so I approached through a different unit before climbing the fence between them. The trickiest bit was at the top, trying to make sure I balanced my feet in between the barbed wire. Fortunately, not that high a fence.

When I got a foot on top, I could push the wire down. I dropped on the other side, landing in a roll. I wasn't one hundred percent convinced of what I was going to do. This felt very different from what I'd done before. I was reactionary, not like Debbie, everything planned, but this was Jac Moonshine coming out from inside.

Maybe showing off to Kelly, maybe demonstrating to her how I could fight, had upped my ego. After the gym incident, I really was spoiling for the fight. There were no windows on that side of the building, so I had to walk around to the other side, but thankfully, everywhere was in darkness.

The warehouse was purporting to be disused, but after I saw Patrick go in, you could tell that wasn't the case. Maybe it was a hideout. Maybe there were other things in there. I would soon find out. The rear door looked like it didn't close properly, and I sat watching it. After an hour, it opened, and a large man came out looking for a smoke. As he stood puffing on a cigarette, I was wondering how to play this. *Should I attack the man now, incapacitate him? But then if others found him, they would know I was in there. Or did I sneak in? Find out the situation, count how many people were there?*

Part of me wanted to fight straight away. It's a flaw I have. It's vengeance coming through. Take it out on someone, anyone. I chose the wiser course and crept into the warehouse. Once through that first door, I was in a long corridor, several doors leading off it.

I listened. I could hear someone swearing, shouting at someone else. Quickly, I strode along the hall, which led up to several doors. Most of them had glass in them, so you could see inside, but nearly all the rooms were empty. As I got towards the end, there was a door to the left that showed a large warehouse.

There were several boxes in the far corner. I didn't have time to investigate them because brutal sounds were coming from the other door in front of me. Inside, through the glass, I could see someone hanging upside down. Their hands had been tied up behind them, but they were dangling by their feet from what I could make out. There was a pool of blood on the floor. Someone was hitting them repeatedly in the stomach. I watched as they swung back and forward. This must have been Eamon O'Rourke, the poor sod that got blamed for the drugs bust.

I was under the impression that torture never garnered you much information, but if it did, it was what they thought you wanted to hear, not what was the truth. There were at least two men in that room taking turns at him. One was smaller, even smaller than me, but the other was an absolute brute.

I heard a noise from back down the hallway. The door was closing to the outside. The smoker must have finished his smoke. I opened the door into the main warehouse and stepped inside. The smoking man entered the main room where Eamon O'Rourke was swinging, and I wondered how to play this.

I could use my gun. They would surely have guns as well, but I'd never used one in a premeditated action. The guard at the florist was purely reactionary. Did I just walk in and take them down, just shoot them? I took it out of my pocket and looked at it. There was a silencer at the end. Jorge told me it was best to keep that on. Prevented unwelcome attention when you shot someone. In this warehouse, this location, no one outside of the building would hear anything.

The other problem was I didn't know where everyone was in the room, so when I stepped out of my current position, I would have to peer around the door of the main warehouse, trying to look through the other door to find the location of the three men dishing out the treatment to Eamon O'Rourke.

Cracking the door, I could see a man standing. I could open the door and though I'd get a clean shot at him, I would then have to react to the others before they drew weapons. I didn't even know if they had weapons.

There was something that came into my head at that point about a fair fight. Police didn't do this. When the police entered, they gave a warning, and if you then raised your gun, they shot you. I wouldn't. I'd be going in and shooting in cold blood. If they didn't have a gun, they'd be going down anyway.

Burning flowers was one thing. Burning clothing or whatever other racket Randazzo was running was one thing to me. What was bothering me was that this was my endgame, dispatching his people. I needed to see if I could do it. If I couldn't, I should walk now. Walk now, drive home, get Kelly, and just flee. Go to another country.

That was the choice before me within the warehouse. I either went for this as I planned, or I ran. I thought of Alan. We went to run, but we couldn't run quick enough. Could I run and leave it all behind, let these people who had just taken away my life get on with theirs? They'd destroy somebody else's. Would I be teaching Kelly how to run and not stand?

I peered again through the two glass panes into the room inside and watched as they hit Eamon O'Rourke. Inside was burning a hatred. Inside was something that said, were you there? Were you the one that put a bullet in my husband's face?

I didn't wait for the opportune moment. It just came on me like a snap decision. I opened the first door and opened fire. The large man, who was hitting Eamon O'Rourke, got hit twice in the forehead and fell to the ground.

There were no nerves, none. I swung the gun around, catching the next man on the shoulder. The third man I hadn't seen, but he was just in behind the door, and caught me unaware by grabbing my wrist and bending it hard.

The gun fell, but I reared round with my knee, driving it into his side. Then my left fist came up, hitting him. With my hand released, I tore at him, punching and kicking. He fell to the ground, clutching his face. I heard the second man scrambling.

I looked down and grabbed my gun, before turning to see him at the far side of the room, reaching for a weapon. I shot again, twice, three, four times. He lay with only the occasional jerk of his dying spasms. I turned around and looked at the man who had physically grabbed me. He was on the floor moaning. I put two quick shots in his head. During this time, Eamon O'Rourke was screaming. I will not bore you with the language, but I didn't get him down. Instead, I kneeled beside his battered face.

"Stop speaking," I said to O'Rourke. "Stop speaking now." He shut up quickly. I put a gun to his head. "You need to understand what's going to happen. They've blamed you for stealing the drugs that I took. My name's Jac Moonshine," I said.

I took a little bottle of potcheen out of my jacket and started waving it in front of him.

"You're going to deliver this bottle, and you're going to tell them that Jac Moonshine took their drugs, and there's no point looking for them because Jac Moonshine doesn't want them. Jac threw them in the river. What Jac wants is Randazzo, and he's going to come for him, and he's going to take all, and I mean all, of Randazzo's organization. All the flower shops, the clothing, all those targets, that was Jac.

"But Jac knows there are nastier targets behind that, and this is where it starts. I will come for his henchmen, I will come for his organization, and then I will go for his wife, and then him. You're going to pass that on, Eamon, understand? Because if you don't, the first person I come for will be you, and I'll get you to deliver the same message. Only this time, it'll be written on your body bag."

I cut him down and let him walk out of there. When I got back to my car, I realized that the efforts that night had taken a toll, for I was shaking.

Chapter 11

I sat in the car, shaking. There was blood on my clothing. At the time, it didn't seem like it, more like I was detached from it. I fired, I hit someone. I didn't think about what was coming out of them. All I was concerned with was I'd shot him dead. Then the next one I hit on the shoulder. There was blood pooling out underneath Eamon O'Rourke for they beat him good. My knee had gone into that and it had dripped everywhere.

I took the car and burned it out, wrapping the clothes up inside a bag beforehand. But when I got home, the clothes I had changed into also had blood on the inside where it seeped through my disguise onto my skin. It's the first time I realized just how messy everything could get.

When I arrived home, I went straight up to the shower, thankfully not dropping anything on the way. Once in there, I locked the door, going over in my head what I had done. The car was burned out, so there shouldn't be anything in there. Eamon O'Rourke was free. All he had to do was drop a bottle off to Randazzo. Once I knew he was alive, I would get hold of Eamon O'Rourke and make sure he worked for me. I would tell him I could still drop him in it, but it might just be Randazzo's thing to finish him when he gave the message.

I changed out of my clothes, putting them into the bag with the Jac Moonshine outfit. There was lots of blood inside there. It had got onto the bathroom floor, but at least everything was contained inside. I stepped into the shower underneath the warm jets of water and watched as it turned pink, flowing down into the plug hole. I took a lump of shower gel down to my knees, washing off where I had kneeled down in O'Rourke's blood.

It felt like I had to keep washing, over and over, but the stain was not coming out. It's the Lady Macbeth feeling all over again. I shook as I stood in the shower. Going through my head were those faces. The three of them were beating Eamon O'Rourke to a pulp. Any of them could have put the gun into Alan's face and yet I still felt a sense of regret, a sense of remorse.

No, this was right. They needed to be ended. Randazzo needed to suffer. I didn't kill O'Rourke, or had I? *Did sending him back to Randazzo kill him? Would it? If he even made it there. He could barely walk as he left that warehouse. Maybe I should have torched it as well. I didn't know if that would have been the thing to do.*

Of course, I shot the three of them. They'd find the bullets, so the gun had to go too. I needed to take it away, bury it deep somewhere no one was going to find it, and then get myself a new one. That was wise, just in case I got caught. I didn't know. I'd not done this before. I'd not been so brutal before. It was definitely a change-up.

Thump, thump, thump. There was a knock on the shower room door. "Are you in there?" It was Kelly.

"Yes. What's the matter?"

"I've been thinking about this. Why do you let them come around? Why do you let Randazzo in here?"

"Why? What do you mean, why? It's not like I can stop him, is it?"

"Do you even try? Are you just letting him? I saw him in the gym. He beat that guy for touching me, but he was all over you. I saw him."

"Are we having this now?" I said. "Are we really having this now? I'm in the shower. I think this is more of a sit-down-properly discussion."

"I'm not doing that," she said. "How can you let him? Da's dead, you know. There are rumors you hear."

"What rumors?" I ask.

"They killed him, didn't they? Randazzo's lot killed him."

"You don't know that," I said, but she was right. She was totally right.

"But he could have done it," said Kelly, "and there's you letting him do what he wants to you. Has he been to bed with you yet?"

"No, he has not! Don't you ever think I'll be there. Don't you ever think . . ."

"How am I meant to think?" shouted Kelly loudly. "How? Come out here now and tell me."

She meant it as well. She meant it and there's me standing in the shower, pink water running down into the sinkhole, disappearing. I wasn't clean. If I stepped out, I'd still have blood marks on my legs. I had to take my time with this. I just couldn't walk out.

"I'm having a shower," I said.

"What do you mean? You're telling me you can't come and speak to me just because you're in the shower? This is important, Mum. What do you mean?"

"In the morning. In the morning, Kelly, we'll talk. Okay?"

There was a sudden kicking of the door and then she disappeared, stomping off so that the floorboards resonated through to me. I stood and put my head back, letting the water hit my forehead, roll down over my shoulders, my chest, down along my legs until it hit my feet. I turned the tap, so it became slightly warmer.

When I used to get worked up like this, Alan would rub my shoulders, he'd work my back, and then possibly we'd even work out together. He was my foil, my counterpart, the one who sustained me. He was my calm in the middle of the storm. Now he was gone.

I didn't blame Kelly, but she really could have picked a better time. I needed to head back out again. I needed to burn the bag because I couldn't really clean it. I also had to get the bag downstairs to the washing machine and throw the clothes in a hot wash, including the Jac Moonshine outfit. *Or should I go out to a launderette? Would that be better?* I had absolutely no idea.

Taking them out was an instinctive thing. The pressure was building; I needed to lay down a marker. I thought somehow it would be cleaner, easier. You see it in the movies, don't you? You walk in; you shoot this one; you shoot that one. Sometimes there's a hundred who die before they get to the key person, and all the while they're just rolling around looking wonderful.

I looked and felt a mess, but thankfully, I'd been good at what I did. I got lucky with the third one. He made a grab for my wrist. With any sense, he'd have struck me in the head, made me stumble back, lose my bearings for a moment, then the gun would've come away easily. I got lucky in some ways because I got someone stupid.

I stood there as long as I ever had in a shower, possibly over half an hour, and the water just kept coming down. I understood Kelly's anger. It must look strange when I'm appeasing Randazzo, but I have a limit. If he ever tries to take me to bed, I'll kill him there and then. I'm not becoming that woman.

Eventually, I stepped out of the shower to look back at it and see the blood that's in it. There're stains and they're going to take cleaning. I needed to do it that evening. I wrapped myself in my dressing gown, opened the door and saw Kelly storming along the hallway towards me. I closed the shower room door quickly behind me.

"Come with me," said Kelly, grabbing me by the arm. She dragged me down the stairs and all I can think of is how I've got a bloody bag up in that shower and a load of blood still around the walls of the shower. It needs cleaned before she enters it again.

As we reached the ground floor, she hauled me into the kitchen. It was the first time I'd seen it since I was out at the restaurant. On the table was an enormous bunch of flowers.

"Read that," says Kelly. "Bloody well read that." There was a big card among the flowers. It was white and had some gold trim as well. In the middle, it said, "I'll be your protector," signed Randazzo, or rather it's signed Dazzo. It must have been how he saw himself. Was it his lady's name to call him? I didn't know.

"Look at that," said Kelly. She points to another set of flowers, not as big as the last, and reached for the card, looking at it. It had the same white background with the gold leaf trim around it, and on it, it said, "My apologies, Kelly, a true beauty with curves like your mother."

"Did you read that?" said Kelly. "Did you read that? Who says that about someone's daughter—who?"

She was totally correct, of course. It was ridiculous. Why would you deliver two sets of flowers, one to the mother and another one saying, "Oh, by the way, your daughter's just as good looking." I wondered what he had in store for us in the long run. I was sure that was where Kelly was coming from. She must have been scared witless.

She was at that age where some girls become women, but sometimes only in the body and not in the mind. She was too young to understand the wiles of other people, and yet not so young as to not attract them.

Kelly reached over, grabbed the flowers, and marched to the front door.

"Where are you going?" I said, but she was out the door before me. When I reached it, I saw her at the bin, throwing the flowers in the trash. She was marching back in for mine.

"Don't," I say. "Don't."

"You can't keep these here. It's an affront to Da. Two fingers up to Da."

"Listen, Kelly," I said. "Listen carefully. This man is dangerous. If he comes back, I want him to see these here. I want him to get the idea that I'm okay with it."

"Why?" raged Kelly. "Why?"

"Because I need to keep you safe, that's why. He already told me to keep you in line at the funeral. He told us at a damn funeral, Kelly. If he's going to do that, who knows what else he'll do? Who knows?" There was a knock at the door, but it was open, for Kelly had stormed back in. The spindly figure of Detective Frogg stood in the doorway.

"My apologies," he said, "for coming in at such an inopportune time. I couldn't help but hear the commotion that was going on. Is everything okay?"

"Of course, it's not okay," said Kelly.

I raised my finger to her, "Shush, Kelly."

"Why shush? Why should I? I've got nothing to hide from him."

"There's a pleasant set of flowers out in the trashcan," said Frogg. "From anyone in particular?"

"They're from Randazzo," I said, "but Kelly doesn't appreciate hers."

"Well, I think the lady's got some taste. I see he gave you a bigger set. What you had to do to deserve those, who knows?"

I stepped forward, ready to give the man a slap around the cheeks, but Kelly chipped in first.

"That's what I've told her. That's what I've told her."

"You know he wants you," said Frogg. "I can get you out of here, but I need information."

"I don't have any information," I said. "I know you don't like who Alan used to work with. None of us do, but detective, understand this. Alan worked on the clean side of the business, at least that which was legitimate. He didn't get involved in the other side. He had to be clean so he could stand up and defend the legitimate side. I know what Randazzo is though."

"Do you?" said Frogg. "Do you really? Mrs. Parlor, it'll start with you—always does. It's like he conquers some other man's woman, but it won't be enough. Don't take this the wrong way, miss," said Frogg, turning to Kelly, "but you've got a figure that the likes of Randazzo will want, and he won't stop until he gets it. He has a wife, but that's only for show. That man, a lot of these men, they don't stop there. Then once they've got you, they keep you. You'll be second rate, though; you'll be their piece of good-looking flesh. You'll be there for whatever their wives don't give them. You'll have to do whatever they say. Sad way to be, but they put a gun to your head if you don't. Dispose of you, get rid of you. Randazzo is not just bad news; he's much worse than that."

"Don't you worry about me," I said. "I can handle Randazzo."

"No, you can't," said Kelly. "No, you can't."

"I hope I haven't disturbed your preparations for going out with him," said Frogg.

"No," I said. "I don't understand where you're coming from. I'm just having a shower before bed. I'm not going anywhere near him."

"Just as well," said Frogg. "I think he's kind of busy tonight. He'll be pissed."

"Why?" I asked.

"Somebody took three of his men out. Apparently, they were giving attention to someone who then ran off. I heard he's exploded. He's doing his nut over whatever has happened. I haven't got close to him yet, but I will. I'll pull him in. You don't have to worry about that.

"Nasty incident today as well, wasn't it? I mean at the gym. Oh, he has all the managers well trained, but they must have kicked the living daylights out of that guy in front of you. He likes to do that. He likes to show himself to be tough in front of a woman, so she gets the hint. They don't walk away. Once you're involved with them, that's it. There's only one way out."

I felt my hands shaking, so I kept them behind me as the detective kept talking.

"Still, maybe it's better to keep those flowers there. You don't know how off the handle he'd go. Anyway, I thought I'd warn you in case you went out with him tonight. Seems to be around you a lot lately."

"Not by choice."

Frogg laughed. "A choice. As if you have a choice. No, like you say, it's not by your choice." He turned and walked back to the open door. "I'll shut this for you. Keep the cold out." Once he shut the door, Kelly looked over at me.

"Is that what you want to be? Do you want to be a whore for him? You want to be a hooker for Randazzo? Let's run," said Kelly. "Let's run and get out of here. We could go back to Ireland. Why can't we go to Ireland?"

For a moment, the image sounded good. I could see the green fields. I could see the stone walls. I could see the sea at the coast and the rain coming over it to the land in waves, and then I thought, *No. I must avenge Alan. Alan has to be avenged. They ended him like he was nothing. The man needs to understand just what he was, how much he was to me.*

I stepped towards Kelly, put my arms out, but she turned from me and walked away. "You're just making no sense, Mom," she said. "You make no sense to me at all."

I watched her stomp away and lock herself inside her bedroom. I disappeared into the back room, pull out some cleaning utensils, and make my way up to the shower. I didn't switch it on. Instead, I used the sink inside the room, filled it up with a decent quality bleach, and then scrubbed down the shower room. I was over an hour in there, but by the time I finished, there wasn't a trace of blood. I remember thinking how easy it was to tidy it all away.

I returned the products to where they belonged before going to bed. The sooner the night was over, the better. Lying in bed, I suddenly realized how big it was. I'd been sleeping there for how long since Alan died, yet it was only then that I appreciated the size of it, the loneliness of it. Having had a day like that, I would've sat in bed with Alan and talked to him, listened to his replies, but mostly curled up in his arms.

Alan—I owned him and they took him away from me. I was going to take away what they owned before I took away what they were. The first I'd do for vengeance. The second I'd do for myself.

Chapter 12

When I look back on it all, I think that night after those first killings, the time I freed Eamon O'Rourke, that first night, I played it wrong. I should have taken Kelly up on her offer. We should have run. I should have gotten her established somewhere, and then in a couple of years, I should have come back on my own, unknown, and changed it all. Randazzo wouldn't have forgotten Alan in a couple of years, and he certainly wouldn't have forgotten me when I appeared in front of his face with a gun.

I also didn't realize that anger was running deep within Kelly, and it wasn't at me. I was just the person she could shout at. I was just the person she knew wouldn't fight back. She was angry at her Da too. Why was he involved with people like this? She couldn't have a go at him; he'd died after all, and now she realized it had been the people he was working for that did it. Things spiraled from that point. My laid-out plan hit a bump, so that everything ramped up, and it was Kelly that did it.

But first I better catch you up. Eamon had gone back to Randazzo and had given him the bottle. When I next went into the restaurant, the name of Jac Moonshine was mentioned several times. I tried not to smile as the old woman I was portraying never smiled, but when I left, I grinned. Jac was becoming a pain in the neck.

I followed up on this success, even escalating the warehouse action, setting fire to shipments of goods here and there. Then I realized I was simply resorting to what I knew, retreating, not going forward. I got hold of Eamon O'Rourke.

I caught him one night coming out of a club, stood in front of him with the full Jac Moonshine outfit, and told him he was going to work for me.

He laughed and said, "Why would I do that?"

I said, "Because if you don't, I'm going to drop a rumor that you worked with me and that's why I saved you."

I told him either way he was working for me. Dead or alive, he would work for me. He came to see my point of view because I told him I didn't want him to kill anyone. I didn't want him to do anything out of the ordinary. I just wanted him to phone me. I'd set up a mobile number with pay-as-you-go, something hard for him to trace.

I gave him set times to phone me, little five-minute windows when I knew I'd be alone, Kelly would be out, and he started to call. He gave me details of where certain drug shipments would be, gave me details of rackets that were being played on other people, nightclubs that were owned by Randazzo. I set fire to a few. I took out some drug dealers; I hurt him. It was all going so well until I got that phone call.

"Jac, Eamon. I was going to tell you to come down to one of Randazzo's joints tonight. There is a drug deal going on in the back, but something's come up."

"What do you mean, something's come up?"

"There's this girl. She can only be about seventeen or

eighteen. She's taken a gun and gone into one of Randazzo's joints. I heard a couple of shots. I went inside, but it looks like they have taken her into the back room."

"Somebody's had a go on Randazzo?" I asked.

"Yes," he said. "As far as I understand it, it's the daughter of that guy, Alan. Alan Parlor."

My heart sank. Kelly had got a gun? Kelly had gone to shoot Randazzo? How? Kelly had gone to the cinema with friends. That's what she had told me. I stopped and checked myself.

I'd let her down. She believed Randazzo had killed her father, and in that she was correct. From her point of view, he was about to take me over as well and then possibly her. I'd unwittingly backed my daughter into a corner, and now here she was coming out of it. Who knows where she got the gun from? It didn't matter. I tried not to sound agitated on the phone.

"And she's gone inside? What's happened to her?"

"I think they're holding her in the back room. I can't really get in. What should I do?"

"Call her mother," I said. "Call her mother. I want to see if she can get her out first. I'm not a completely wild one; she's an innocent. It's better if she's out of there before I go in."

From the time I hung up the call until thirty seconds later, when Eamon called the house, I tried to compose myself. It wasn't easy; they had Kelly. I'd lost Alan, and now they had Kelly. More than that, how would I get her out? I thought if I went down as Debbie, I thought if I went down and got into the back room, Randazzo might help. I could call him, that's the other thing I could do, but he said last time I needed to control Kelly, and if I didn't . . .

The phone rang, and I picked it up as calmly as I could.

"You don't know me," said a voice on the other end, "and my name isn't important. Your daughter has just gone into one of Randazzo's joints. She had a gun, was firing at people, and now they've taken her inside. She's not coming back out. She's in big trouble, lady. You need to do something."

I shouted hysterically, before I put the phone down. It was probably one of the easiest acts I've had to do because inside of me somewhere there was a mother who was in pain, but I needed to act.

I got hold of the Jac Moonshine outfit, stuck it in the car, and drove down to the address Eamon gave me. A few blocks out, I took the outfit and stuffed it in a bin. When I arrived at the joint, I got out shouting, banging on the door, screaming to be let into the joint, but there was no answer. I went across the road, bought a six-pack of bottled beer, and started flinging the bottles at the outside of the club. Suddenly, the door opened, and a rather large man stood looking at me. His neck was thick, his arms wider than you could imagine.

"What the hell are you doing, woman? Get out of here."

"You've got my Kelly. You throw her out here and I'll go. Until then, I'm not going anywhere."

"Your daughter pulled a gun on us; I don't think she's coming out soon." The man looked left and right just in case there were any cops about, I reckoned.

"I've got Randazzo's ear, so you phone him. You tell him." The man picked up his mobile, dialed a number and then said, "Mr. Randazzo, please. Yes, it's Jake."

I stood looking at him, but the man looked too confident. It's like he knew what would happen. He'd seen it all before. One of the Randazzo's older guards.

"Right, Mr. Randazzo," he said into his phone, and then he

closed down the call. Jake looked up at me with an evil grin and smiled.

"Mr. Randazzo says you can go to hell. He told you to get her to behave. He'll teach her by leaving her with us. If she comes out in the morning, she'll understand what she's to do."

I ran at him, arms swinging like some lunatic, but he put a palm out, pushing me off.

"Don't go to the cops, lady, or she's dead."

I sat on the ground weeping, until he closed the door, and then I banged it several times, kicking and screaming at it, until he opened it again and told me to clear off or he'd break my own arms. I limped away, weeping, until I got round the corner and then I ran for the car. I drove and picked up the Jac Moonshine suit, parked my car up, and then wandered the streets until I found another car behind one nightclub, one of the posher ones using a valet service, where they left the keys in them. The valet boy was easy to knock out and given my mood, I thought I did well to only hit him as hard as I needed to.

I picked up a small convertible. I wouldn't need it for long. I had the suit on, the blonde hair hanging out the back, the mask drawn across my face, the black outfit with the red tie band around it. Jac Moonshine was going to make a statement.

I'd replaced my previous weapon and checked I had loaded it as I drove back to the address Eamon O'Rourke had given me. I saw again the door at the front and I stopped the car a little down the street. The place was eerily quiet.

I banged on the door loudly, turned and ran, and got back in the car. The engine was still running. Jake opened the door, then stepped out, looking to see who had caused the commotion. I put my foot to the floor, and the car sped up quickly. He thought at first that I was trying to run him over and so ran back into the club. I saw his look of horror over his shoulder as he saw me spinning the wheel so the car and I aimed at the door he'd come through.

I hit him before he got inside. The car piled in, causing bricks to fall around me, part of the wall having come down. I was able to open the car door and get out, clambering across the bonnet into the building.

Jake was on the floor and didn't look like he was moving. A man put his head up from behind the bar but threw himself back down when he saw my raised gun. There were two other men in that front room, both on the ground from the commotion of the car crashing in. I fired a shot at one, tagging him, then at the second, clipping him as well. Then I heard a yell.

The man from behind the bar was getting up. He made a mistake in warning me, and I threw myself back behind the car as a shotgun was fired. It only took me a moment to get turned back up and peer over the top of the car to see the shotgun was about to be dispensed again. I ducked back down, let him shoot, then stood up, knowing he'd have to reload.

I fired one shot, catching him in the shoulder. As I passed the man on the ground, who I had already tagged, I put another in his head, followed by finishing the other goon beyond him. Running to the end of the bar, I saw the barman who had wielded the shotgun lying on the floor, trying to reload it. But I'd hit him badly, and he couldn't. I put him out of his misery.

I turned to the door that led deeper into the club. It was locked, so I shot the fixture, kicked the door open, and then threw myself back as somebody shot through. I poked my head round the corner again, saw somebody trying to reload a gun.

Or maybe it was jammed. Either way, it didn't bother me as I stepped into the room and shot.

There were two doors off from there. One may have headed up into the club, but I knew which one the man had been guarding. I walked up to it, kicked it hard with my gun pointed in front of me. The door swung open, and I saw only one man inside, but he was holding all the cards. He was bald, maybe six feet, and he had a gun pointed at the head of my daughter. Kelly had her hands tied behind her back. Her eyes were dripping tears, her hair a mess, and she was wearing only her bra and knickers. Maybe I had got there early enough. Maybe that was the worst they'd done to her.

"Who are you?" demanded the man.

"Moonshine," I said, and with my spare hand, I took a bottle out of my jacket and rolled it across the floor to him. Slowly, he bent down, the gun still pointed at Kelly's head, and he picked up the bottle. He nodded, saw the label with Jac Moonshine written across it, a tiny figure dressed as I was.

"What's in these?" he asked.

"Usually it's the finest hooch, as you would call it, potcheen. It's made well. Quite the recipe. I've left a few for Mr. Randazzo. Unfortunately, he didn't seem to think it was me. He thought it was Eamon O'Rourke. Crazy talk," I said. "Crazy talk."

"Well, you're too late for this one," said the man. "Randazzo's not happy with her. He's not happy with that bitch mother of hers either. He doesn't like people he wants to play with who don't oblige. He'd still get rid of her, lovely as she is."

The man reached forward, ran a hand down across Kelly's chest. The hand still held the bottle, though. I couldn't shoot. He was too close to her. I needed to wait for him to step back.

"He'll be here any minute. You don't cause this sort of commotion without being told on. They'll be racing down here."

"You won't be leaving though," I said to him. "You realize that, don't you? You're going to let the girl go."

"You must be joking. Randazzo will come down here himself for her. Come and teach her a lesson. It'll put her mother in her place as well."

"What's she to you? Let her go and maybe I'll let you live and tell him."

"O'Rourke got lucky," said the man. "You don't go telling Randazzo bad news like that. He'd just as soon kill you. As for this bottle of hooch, you can just stick it."

The man moved his arm back, ready to toss it over to me. I watched and by the time it had left his hand, I fired a single shot at the bottle.

Because things had escalated, I had taken to carrying a few incendiaries around with me and the easiest thing to store them in was the bottles that I also used for the hooch. It wasn't hooch inside this one. It was a much more potent cocktail.

As the bullet struck the glass, it ignited, causing a brief distraction. The man's eyes were blinded by a bright flash, vapor burning. I had the wisdom, however, to keep mine closed, and as I opened them, I aimed my gun and put two bullets straight into his forehead. He fell straight to the floor, his gun mercifully falling away from Kelly.

I ran forward, picked her up under one of her arms. She was screaming. She couldn't walk either, but I dragged her out onto the street where several people were now gathering, albeit at a distance.

I slipped the gun behind me and continued to drag Kelly

over to a person on the street, placing her in front of them.

"Take care of her and make sure she goes to the cops or the ambulance."

Then I had a sudden thought. I had left no one alive. How would Randazzo know it was Jac? I walked back to the smashed car buried in the wall and placed a Jac Moonshine bottle on the trunk.

I ran off out of sight of the crowd, disappearing through back alleys until I reached my car. Once there, I took off the Moonshine suit. There was blood this time, though not as much as at the rescue of Eamon O'Rourke. There was no blood to kneel in. However, Kelly's face had been a picture, as she'd got covered in the mess of shooting the man that had held her.

I stashed the suit inside an old disused building and then jumped into my car. I took a moment to brush my hair to look reasonably neat, and then I drove back to the scene. I saw Randazzo arrive. I saw a man and a woman holding onto Kelly and the ambulance arriving. Randazzo was walking over to her, but I got there ahead of him.

"I'm her mother," I said. "Let's go."

An ambulance man put us both inside their vehicle and off we went. As he closed the doors, I saw the look from Randazzo. He was raging. The only question was, was he raging at me, Debbie, or me, Jac Moonshine? Or maybe it was both.

Chapter 13

I'll tell you right now, I didn't think once about the men in that establishment. I didn't think once about what had happened to them; all I cared about was I got Kelly back. They were dead. All of them were dead, and they deserved it. I guess in that moment, Jac Moonshine truly took over.

Prior to that, everything I was doing came at a risk. There was a nervousness; there was a feeling inside that I was some fraud pretending I was an avenging angel.

I always thought that I couldn't get angrier than when Alan was killed. I couldn't get angrier than when I was standing in the kitchen being fondled over. A dead man's widow. But then they came for my daughter. They say that about women, don't they? That's our young! We will defend our brood. A woman doesn't know how to kill until she becomes a mother. You suddenly have something that consumes you. It's your own, and you'll fight tooth and nail for them. More than that, we'll tear people apart for them.

I don't know if men ever get how strong that is. Randazzo's men got to understand what it meant, or at least they saw the fury of it. Looking back, I'm stunned by how thoughtful I was during the actions. It wasn't a rashness, a craziness that set in. You see that so often, people going over the top, but never in a position to deal with the situation in front of them. Just lashing out at it. No, I dealt with it and I dealt with it well.

Kelly slept in the next morning. I didn't. I got up, went for a run. There was so much wound up inside me, so much anger and hate that it had to come out. It had to be put somewhere because I know from my martial arts training that if you don't channel it, if you don't let it come out in the right way, you make mistakes. I could make a mistake from my inexperience, but I wouldn't make a mistake letting my emotions get the better of me.

I pounded the streets for some six or seven miles before I came back to the house, and as I did so, I saw a car parked outside I recognized. Part of me wanted to run up to that car, smash the window, take the man inside apart, rip him in two, hold him up for all the world to see. But I had time. You can see down our street for a good thirty seconds when you're running, so by the time I reached the car, I was composed. Eddie Tumbler got out of the front passenger seat and waved me down.

"Mr. Randazzo would like a word with you." I watched as he rounded the car and opened the rear passenger door.

"In there?"

"In here." It was a different tone from Eddie, one that made me wary. Sometimes when they come round and they're all macho and trying to win you and own you, there's a gentleness to the voice. It's the gentleness of a snake, though, creeping up on you. It's not to be trusted.

This was worse. This was a wounded animal snarling back, but inside, something in me lifted. I'd hurt them. I'd really hurt them this time. This wasn't the florist gone ablaze. I didn't destroy some warehouse. I didn't turn around and take some of his drug money, which, no doubt, was an inconvenience. No, this one was different.

This one showed his men could not hold their own. This was his will challenged and tossed aside by someone he didn't know. Someone he was struggling to identify. At least I hope they hadn't found out who it was. That thought crossed my mind as I stepped into the car, but I was too far gone by then.

"You're very lucky, Deborah," said Randazzo, as I sat down beside him. "Very lucky indeed. I told you to take care of your daughter. I told you to keep her in check and she came down waving a gun, and then someone came for her. Have you had anyone round here? Has she been seeing anyone?"

"She's not seeing anyone," I said. "We have had no one here. Who's going to come here knowing that you're looking after me? You made it clear at the gym. Plenty of people saw that."

"Evidently not enough," said Randazzo. "Your little girl should be dead, except I like you, Debbie. The fact she's come back to you is a gift."

A gift? I thought. *A gift? My daughter's life is a gift. He took her into the place. He blew the head off her father in front of her eyes, and he talks about giving me a gift.*

The one thing I realized more and more as I went along was how these people were not just simply deluded. They're almost psychotic. Sometimes I sit and think, *Maybe I could reason this out. Maybe I could come to a deal. Maybe there'd be a place to coexist, but there isn't.* There isn't when they're like this. How do you make rational decisions with someone who talks about giving your daughter back to you as a gift? It was his fault she ran after him with a gun.

"Do you know who saved her?"

"No," I said lying. "I got down there. I brought her home. I don't know. I know nothing."

His hand went up to my face. "Debbie," he said, "you've got to take better care of her. You've got to keep her on a leash. It's only because I'm so fond of you." I watched as he ran his eyes up and down my body. *He wasn't fond of me. It was more like having a dog,* I thought, *or maybe more like a prized necklace sitting out on display.* Look at what I wear. Debbie was only a fashion accessory.

"Somebody called Jac, Jac Moonshine, came for her. I don't know who he is, but I will. Gimmicky name, anyway."

Who he is, I thought, *wonderful. Who he is.* Randazzo cursed when he said Jac Moonshine again.

"I'm telling you this out here because we're going to go in and have a word with her. You're going to tell her she's not to come after the people who are protecting you and her. We're going to make clear that next time she won't be so lucky."

Randazzo indicated I should go to the house, and the door was opened for me. I stepped out of the car to a faint smile from Eddie Tumbler. He never looked good; after all, he had a deep scar on the side of his face, but Eddie was also on his best behavior. I only got a faint smile. No attempt to escort me, no attempt to lay a finger on me. That was done by Randazzo. He walked around the side of the car and his hand went to my hip. It soon descended. I opened the front door and Randazzo followed me through.

"Where is she?" he asked.

"She's probably not up yet." I went to stop him as he climbed the stairs, but there was no holding him back. He was going to see Kelly, whatever.

"Which door?" he asked as we reached the top of the stairs,

and I pointed over. It was a simple wooden door on the outside. You couldn't have told which of us slept in which room from the outside, but as soon as it was opened, there was the usual teenage paraphernalia of posters and the odd, soft, cuddly toy.

He walked over to where Kelly was lying under a duvet. He whipped it back quickly, and I heard her scream. For a moment, I thought she'd gone to bed without dressing. Then I realized she was in her pajamas but still felt exposed. She'd grabbed the duvet back, sitting with scared eyes, looking at him. And who could blame her? The man's goons were looking to kill her the previous night.

"You need to listen, and you need to listen well. What you did last night usually means the death of someone, and it should've been you. You don't come at my people with a gun. I don't know what cock and bull story you are thinking of. I don't give a shit who you think I killed or didn't kill. I'm looking after you and your mom now, so you'd better get with it, girl, because if you don't, it'll only be your mom I'm looking after."

As if to enforce the point, Randazzo whipped an arm around me, pulled me close, and kissed me in front of her. Not a subtle kiss. It was deep. His hands roaming down my back, there to demonstrate that he owned me.

"From now on, I'm going to have somebody outside the house to look after you. Wherever you go, somebody will follow you because if I find out that the person who saved you knows you, I'll kill you, Kelly. You understand? I will kill you, and it won't be a quick death either."

Kelly was huddled up in a ball, the covers pulled up tight around her. Her face was white, tears streaming down her face. I went to go to her, but Randazzo grabbed me by the wrist.

"No, no," he said. "She needs to feel this. She needs to know the fear. Maybe I'll get a good man in your life. Let one of the boys get close to you, Kelly. Be able to put you on a tight leash. Keep control over you like I control your mom."

With that, he smacked me hard on the backside. My fist clenched up quickly, and I had to fight to unclench it in what was a very unnatural movement. Maybe that was good though, because it looked like I was scared. It looked like I wasn't treating this as if it was something that just had to happen, but it had to happen. Randazzo needed to be convinced that I was Debbie. Scared, weak Debbie.

He stepped forward towards Kelly, went down on one knee in front of her and said, "Do you know Jac Moonshine?"

Kelly shook her head.

"See, she doesn't," I said. "I told you."

"Shut the hell up," Randazzo said to me suddenly. He turned back to Kelly. "Are you sure?" Kelly nodded. He smacked her with the back of his hand, a blow that would've jarred me. But for eighteen-year-old Kelly, it was like she'd been hit with a hammer. Her head spun off to the left, and she collapsed down onto the bed, tears streaming. When she sat back up, I saw blood coming from her mouth. Again, I went to reach for her, but Randazzo grabbed me.

"Just bloody stand there or I'll give you some of the same."

He had his back to me. If truth be told, I thought about stepping up behind him, putting my arms around his neck and twisting it, killing him right there and then. Of course, all his goons were outside. I couldn't escape. I couldn't get away with it. There were only the three of us in the room, but part of me edged towards him. Randazzo never saw me. I was right behind him. Then the doorbell went.

"Who the hell's that?" raged Randazzo. Then his phone

went off. He picked it up and looked at it. "Bloody detective downstairs. You listen to me, Kelly, you listen good. You interfere in my affairs again, you are dead. Dead. There won't be a warning."

Randazzo turned and grabbed me by the wrist and hauled me out of the room. "Get down there to that bloody door." The doorbell was ringing again. I hurried down the stairs, pulled back the door to see Detective Frogg standing there.

"What the hell are you doing here?" asked Randazzo.

"Checking up on last night's victim. What happened to your men?"

Frogg was thin and looked like a stick compared to Randazzo's bulk, but he stood his ground as Randazzo loomed towards him.

"You just catch the damn killer that finished them. Do your bloody job."

"I'm doing my job. We had a child kidnapped last night, held by people. I'd like to question them, but I can't. They're not around anymore."

"Don't get involved in shit you can't handle," said Randazzo suddenly. Frogg showed absolutely no emotion.

"Anyway, what are you doing here?" asked Frogg.

"Just looking after a former friend's wife. After all, her daughter had a bit of a shock last night. Not sure what happened in there. Don't think she knows either. Either way, she's not very well at the moment."

"That true?" asked Frogg to me.

"Of course, it's bloody true," snarled Randazzo.

I gave a faint nod.

"Don't waste your time around here, detective," said Randazzo. He kissed me several times right in front of the detective before walking out the door. I saw most of the cars drive off, but one was remaining outside the house.

"Strange choice of lover," said Frogg.

"You have two errors in that statement," I said. "One, lover. Two, choice."

"Have you heard anything about a Jac Moonshine? Apparently Jac's leaving messages, small bottles behind. Randazzo is quite spooked. Can you confirm that?"

"I confirm nothing. Randazzo owns me. You've seen that. I'm just glad I got my girl out last night. Need to teach her some sense, how to handle these people."

"Sounds like somebody is handling them," said Frogg.

I heard stomping down the stairs, turned and saw Kelly, and Frogg gave a tip of his hat as she stood beside me. She said nothing, but slapped me across the face.

"He was damn well threatening me. He threatened me, Mom, and you just took it. You let him kiss you, kiss you while he was . . ."

"And do what? What was I meant to do? Turn around and fight him?"

"Jac Moonshine would've fought him. Jac Moonshine came for me last night; it wasn't my mom. No. Some random person."

It was hard not to stand there and tell Kelly who it was. I was there. I looked after you. I couldn't do it in front of Frogg anyway, but the difficulties of getting Kelly to listen at the best of times were now well surpassed.

"Listen, kid," said Frogg. "Your mother's walking a tough line here. You could have ended up dead last night. Don't go taking a gun to these punks again. It's not worth it. You'll just give your mother a very expensive funeral. I think the two of you are probably in way over your head. I can try to get you a way out. I can try to . . ."

"Where the hell were you guys?" yelled Kelly. "What did the police do when my Da got shot? Bugger all, bugger all. You can piss off." She turned and marched back up the stairs.

"Whoa. Feisty one. You're a lot quieter though, aren't you?" he said to me.

"I have my moments," I said quietly, "and I think you should leave. Randazzo's left men outside and if you're here for over ten minutes, they're going to put two and two together and get five, and that puts us at risk."

"Of course," and Frogg tipped his hat and closed the door behind him.

Things had been set in motion. Kelly had entered the fray. Randazzo was jumping up and down. Everything was getting too complex, too tied up together. Too much involvement from too many sides. I thought revenge would be easy. A slow-burn process where I would pour on the pain bit by bit. Instead, it had to be something quicker, something to the heart. Well, he had killed my spouse, hadn't he? I decided it was time to look at Randazzo's wife.

Chapter 14

Have you ever been watched? I mean properly watched. It's an absolute pisser. Eddie Tumbler was running cover on our house. If I went out for a jog, he stopped me. If I stepped outside of the house, he came over to say hello. Either him or one of his goons.

The worst of it was at two in the morning when he banged on the door like the flood was about to happen. I jumped out of bed, threw on a gown, and came down. He was just checking that I was still in the house. The thing that got me was as soon as he saw I was down in just my dressing gown, he insisted on coming in. Then I had half an hour of Eddie trying to take over from Randazzo, but without saying it, trying to get a little something on the side.

You end up playing that cat-and-mouse thing. If it would have been me as Jac, then I would have broken his neck. But because it's Debbie, I feign the inability to deal with the situation. I sit there and take a little abuse. But it's all part of the game. It's all part of them seeing this weak woman. All part of making sure they don't see the tsunami arrive.

Every time Eddie Tumbler touched me, I told myself how I would kill him. Each time was different. Some of these thoughts took me to places that I didn't think I could go to. Taking knives to parts of them I think, *When did I become like that?* Then I remember they threatened my daughter. They killed my husband. They treated me like I was some piece of meat. Detective Frogg kept coming around and he was nosing and trying to find a way in, but trying to find a way into Randazzo's defenses was difficult.

The other frustration of being watched was that Jac Moonshine still had to get things done. I planned shorter missions. I had to think about operating on the hoof. A couple of nights, I would wait until Eddie had made his excuses to come in and then left, then run upstairs, get changed, out the back window, and do something not particularly dastardly. Set fire to something again, small fry.

It wasn't working, though. I needed to be out on the streets properly, with no worries about coming back to find him inside my house, wondering where I'd been. I also couldn't come back to the house in a state. I knew what I was doing was dangerous. If I got caught one night and maybe came back with a serious wound, how would I explain it?

I endured three weeks of Eddie Tumbler until they must have got bored thinking we were under control. Kelly was a pain in the ass. She was constantly going on about Randazzo, constantly shouting at me. I was out to destroy the man, but I couldn't tell her. She was safe and kept away from Randazzo and his men.

Then they left us alone to a large degree. They stopped coming at night. Eddie Tumbler was no longer the one watching the house. It was another man, one I didn't recognize, and he was usually on his own.

Despite this, I decided I needed a base of operations, somewhere away from the house. All superheroes had somewhere away from the house, didn't they? Why couldn't I? Not that I was a superhero, just a vengeful wife.

Oh, I didn't feel bad about it. I didn't feel somehow inferior to a superhero. You always had the superheroes who did everything right. It always worked for them in the comics, didn't it? Or if it didn't, they always made a comeback at some point. I didn't have time to make a comeback. I had to get things done.

It was two in the morning, and I'd snuck out of the house. I was on the south side of the city, down amongst the down and outs, but not that far from where a lot of Randazzo's operations took place. Drugs were rife around here.

I came across a building that I liked the look of. There was a metal door across what had been the entrance, but it wasn't secured in any serious way. Once inside, I stepped across piles of worn-out clothes and scraps of food. I saw some rats run here and there and was sure I could smell urine.

Further into the house, there were stairs up to three floors. There were rooms on each of these floors. Empty. Bare floorboards. Some running water, but not much. No electricity. The place looked like it should be demolished. I also found a basement. More than that, it had fallen through in one part of the house. Therefore, there was a large hole. The second time I visited, I was standing looking down into that hole in the basement when I heard a noise. Someone reached for me from behind. I caught the wrist and jerked the hand hard, bringing them down to the ground.

"Agh. Get off. I'm only . . ."

I saw the homeless man on the floor and let go.

"Who the hell are you?" I asked.

"My friends call me Deck."

"Like Declan?"

"No, I have a deck of cards. They don't. I'm Deck."

Deck stank. I struggled to hold my gaze on him with the odor that was attacking my nose.

"Do you live here, Deck?"

"I do," he said, "mostly. Who are you?"

"I'm Jac," I said. "I'm going to buy this and I'm going to work out of here."

"This is where I live."

"Indeed, it is, Deck. What are you on?" He named a substance I didn't know. "How much do you need a day?"

I know what you're thinking. Here is this junkie, down and out, stuck in a dump like this. I could have turned around and I could have offered him a house and a car just to keep guarding this place for me. I could have offered him money and food. It's not what he wanted. He wanted a bit more of the magic stuff that made everything disappear.

"I can get you plenty of that," I said, "but I need you to do something for me."

"What's that?"

"I need you to live on the bottom floor here. I need you to chase other people away. Not nastily, cleverly. Make sure they disappear."

"Why is that?" he asked.

"Because I need to stash some stuff here. Oh, don't worry. It's not stuff you're going to snuff up your nose or that, but it's important I've got somewhere. You, Deck, are going to be the man that's going to provide that."

In the following days, I found out who the house belonged to. Then I put in an offer for it, one they couldn't refuse. I wasn't shy about money, you see. That was the thing. Alan wasn't stupid. Alan left us well off financially. That house, well, let's just say it wasn't particularly expensive.

Over the coming weeks, I filled the house up. Medical supplies up top. I had somewhere to draw out the schemes that Randazzo was running on a whiteboard. I could start looking and planning about entering his house, too. I set up a computer, and all the while down below, Deck pottered about. I left him food sometimes, and I got Eamon to get me the drugs.

That was interesting. Eamon didn't think he'd see me again, and suddenly, I tracked him down. It wasn't difficult. Eamon O'Rourke wasn't good at hiding his tracks. He wasn't someone that covered them well. He was good as well, good as gold. Picked me up whatever it was Deck was on. Kept feeding it to him. If I needed something that I couldn't get myself, Eamon went out and got it, brought it back to the building.

One thing I got was a motorbike. Hiring cars, changing them over, was a pain in the neck. The house didn't have anywhere I could put a car, but I could hide a motorbike in that basement. A simple piece of wood ran up to the ground floor. You went down the wood when you wanted to put it away, then you went up the wood when you wanted to bring out the bike.

The other thing I did was fill that place with clothes, multiple disguises, men's clothes, women's clothes, whatever I needed. From that building, I could walk out looking like anyone. I set up a large mirror with lights as you would in a theater. Backstage room, Deck called it.

"Your backstage room. Are you going in there?" Then he'd make the same joke every time I came out. "Who the hell is this?"

He used to laugh loud at that. I liked Deck. I liked him a lot.

Part of me wanted to give him a chance back at life, but I'm not sure he would have taken it. He just wanted to shove stuff up his nose. With me being the principal supplier and able to get him it regularly, Deck was keeping me happy.

With the house in full swing, I could carry out other operations on Randazzo. I stopped a couple of his drug deals because I heard Kozlov wasn't coming. I picked up Kozlov's men again, several of them, each time depositing those drugs out into the river. Pretty soon, Mannersberg was up in arms. Somebody was doing the police's job for them.

The public had a mixed view of Jac Moonshine. Oh yes, they liked the fact that Randazzo was getting taken down a peg or two, but they weren't keen on Jac's methods. I thought that was harsh. Jac's methods were suitable. They were effective. They worked. It didn't work if you just pussyfooted around these people.

I also started doing reconnaissance. I went to Randazzo's house. I watched his wife and where she went. It needed to be the right time. I couldn't go after Randazzo's wife and that'd be the end. I had to come back from that one and then go for him. And Kozlov, of course. Kozlov, who ordered Alan's death, told Randazzo that they should kill my man. He only thinks he was offended.

Over the coming months, Jac Moonshine made an appearance, at least on a weekly basis. What impressed me the most was the name rang around the town. Everyone knew the black figure with the red band around their waist. What I found quite interesting was nobody quite knew what Jac's figure was like. I didn't get seen often. What was left was the bottle of hooch.

Randazzo was still visiting the house as well, but he got more edgy. I would let him have his way with me to a point. He'd never get into my bed, but yes, I would let him have me on his lap once in a while. I was out to dinner with him frequently, wearing whatever ridiculous or obscene outfit he bought for me that week. Debbie was the kept woman, the protected woman, but the other side of me was running amok. So much so that one night I turned up at the house to see Deck's puzzled face. I had a cardboard box, and it was clinking as I came in.

"That doesn't sound like any decent stuff."

"Oh, this is decent. This is more than decent," I said. Deck helped me carry the box upstairs, where I put it down and took out lots and lots of small bottles. There were also several labels. I printed them off on the computer and I attached them all to the bottles. Deck sat and worked with me, though his hands were quite shaky.

"That's that man who's been running around, causing that gang lord a lot of trouble," said Deck. "It's not been good. When people like that get annoyed, supply stops, people don't get fed properly. Somebody will get it in the neck," said Deck. "You be careful," he said. "I know you're just looking out for him here and supplying stuff for him. The money might be good, but don't go down the road with these people, these vigilantes. They just cause issues. They just stop supplies of drugs and stuff coming in. Stuff I need."

I gave Deck a smile. For someone who was homeless, someone who was struggling, he seemed to understand how things worked.

He was certainly ever the watchdog. A couple of times I'd been upstairs and seen him chase people off from down below. Because of that, I let him pour my daddy's potcheen into the small bottles. Every now and again, he would take a quick nip of it.

"Hey, that's for the bottles."

"Plenty in the bottles. Plenty in the bottles. Anyway, I doubt he drinks them afterwards, does he? You don't put that to somebody as a, 'Oh, sorry. I've just shot some of your people.'"

I laughed. "No, I don't. You're absolutely right. Anyway, I don't know what Jac does with this. Never met him," I said.

"And I never met you," said Deck.

We sat, filling up the bottles with my Da's hooch, the few bottles I had left of it. This couldn't be too much of a continued campaign because I'd run out of bottles.

"You know where that Jac Moonshine is getting it wrong?" said Deck.

"No," I said. "Enlighten me."

"He's constantly going after Randazzo, everything is done against Randazzo, and they think it's Jac Moonshine. Jac Moonshine needs to take a leaf out of somebody else's book."

"Whose?" I said.

"Mine," said Deck. "When you want to annoy someone, don't annoy them yourself. Set it up so it looks like they've annoyed someone else so another person will have a go at them. So much easier, and if they're really annoyed about it, they won't come after you. They'll come after this other person who reported it."

"You're right," I said, "you're absolutely right." I needed to stop being a fly annoying Randazzo. I needed to become a cancer, something that would break him down by breaking up the trust and the links he had within his organization.

"Good man, Deck," I said. "Good man." I didn't get a reply. I just heard some more hooch disappearing down his throat.

Chapter 15

It was time to bring down Randazzo's organization. Not that it was an arduous task to motivate myself for. His men had carried out the killing of my husband, but if I could get infighting going on between the gangs that were in the city, it would take the heat off Jac Moonshine and also allow me more freedom to track down Randazzo's wife.

The best way to sow distrust and conflict was to look at drugs. There was a hard under core of drug use within the city, probably much like anywhere else, but the money was made by those supplying it to the street dealers. Randazzo was one of those people. Donovan was his big rival.

Randazzo was already annoyed, because Donovan had been taking the supply off Kozlov, and I thought I could play on that. The key thing was to get the timing right. I would need to capture a shipment for Donovan. I would then need to get the shipment into Randazzo's warehouse, and then have Donovan's men find it there.

I could get the drugs shipment, but I wasn't in a place to spread the word. I didn't know all of Donovan's men. I didn't know all Randazzo's men, but Eamon O'Rourke was in a good place for that. He could get the word out for me. Although still wary of me, he was working for me.

The heat around the house had also died down, which meant that although we were watched, the focus was mainly on Kelly. If I went out, it may be noted when I went, but they'd stopped following me. Besides, it was down to one man. If I wanted, I could peel away through the rear of the house without being seen.

Randazzo didn't come around too late at night, having enough to do within his organization. He still popped around during the day, and I maybe saw him two or three times a week. I was wondering just what he was looking for in me. He hadn't forced going to bed, which seemed strange. What was I then?

He would sit and talk; nothing important about the organization, more about him. Why he was stressed, what he was feeling, occasionally cursing Jac Moonshine. Was I a shrink? Was I meant to be his offloading woman? Could he not do that with his wife? Was she just a trophy? Not that any of it mattered to me.

It was just after midnight when I left the house, exiting via the rear door. I caught a cab to the south side of the city and then walked to my new base. Deck was sleeping when I walked in through the old iron door. He opened one eye, muttered something, and then sat up properly when he realized it was me.

"Seen anybody or anything?"

"No," he said, "but those biscuits that came in, don't like them."

"Which ones?" I asked.

"These pink ones."

He threw me a packet. I made a note of the name. That was the thing with Deck. I was doing him a favor, but he could walk out at any time. The little things, they always help. When I saw Eamon, I'd tell him to change the biscuits.

I made my way upstairs and got changed into my Jac outfit. The red band setting off the all-black ensemble. I didn't take any bottles this time, because this wouldn't be me. This would be Donovan's men. That meant that when I took it, I either couldn't be seen or there could be no witnesses. I had a minimal selection of weapons stashed upstairs, and I switched away from the usual handgun I used, taking a baseball bat instead. The gangs tended not to use guns unless they had to. Certainly, the lower levels wouldn't pack any unless approved. And this had to look like something low level.

Eamon O'Rourke told me that Donovan's men also worked out of the south side, but the district they were in was closer to the river. Taking the motorbike out of the cellar, I rode that way until I wound up in a dark street with several streetlamps out. In some ways, it was like where I had just come from. Derelict houses with some boarded-up rooms, the odd light on here and there, but the street was deserted. I parked the bike up in an alley out of the way and took the baseball bat.

I walked casually along some six doors. The five in between were all residents. Ordinary people. They may have been decent; I didn't know. That's the thing about a lot of these neighborhoods. You might get the scum selling the drugs, but you also get ordinary, hardworking people who would love to live somewhere better.

At the sixth door, which was a bright red color, I tapped several times. Eamon O'Rourke, when we were setting up the job, said they would crack the door, waiting for a password to be said. If I was quick, I could stun the person at the door, take them out before they saw me.

I stood quietly, waiting for an answer. A car drove down the street, its lights showing the dark recesses of the street. It turned around the corner and I clocked it, picking up the first digits of the number plate. I knocked on the door again because there was no answer. *Had Eamon O'Rourke given me a dud?*

I could feel myself beginning to sweat now. I didn't like this, being out on the street. I wanted them to just open the door so I could get about my business, but another car came from the opposite direction. I peered at it through the dark, the lights making it difficult to see any features of the car. Only as it got closer did I clock those first three characters of the number plate again. The car was slowing down. The passenger side opened, and someone started to get out. They were a few feet away from me, but it was clear who their target was. The door wasn't opening.

I couldn't see the figure fully as it came round the car door, but that didn't matter. A swing of the baseball bat caught someone on the chin, and they fell down to the ground. Smashing the windscreen with the baseball bat, I pulled the car door open.

Looking inside, I clocked the driver reaching for his glovebox compartment. The baseball bat flew into his chin, and I hit him several times. As I did so, I could hear the door opening behind me at the house. I spun back out of the car with the bat, swung wildly and caught the first person running out of the door across the face.

He fell to one side, and I didn't wait to see who was following him, but turned on my heel, driving the bat into someone's stomach. I dove on their head with the bat, then went back to the first man, hitting him again. There was a lot of painful moaning.

I ran into the house where I could hear chairs being quickly scraped back. I opened the first door to a room and saw my prize. Eamon had said there'd be two black briefcases, and they were sitting on the table. One would be the money being passed over, and the other would be the drugs being delivered. There were two men there. One small and fat, the other leaner.

I didn't wait for the small one who was standing up with a gun. I let go with the bat, my swing catching him on the face, and raced for the other man. He tried to get out of the way, but I grabbed him, pulled his head down and drove a knee up into his face before turning back to the little guy who was on the floor with a bloody nose that poured over his face.

Scanning, I found his gun, picked it up and shot him, before stepping round to the other man, and dispatching him as well. I know it sounds cold, but Jac, she didn't get sentimental.

With a gun having been fired, I ran out of the front door. Two men were still rolling around on the ground, trying to get up. Another sat almost knocked out in the car, but the fourth one was missing. I shot the two on the sidewalk, then the man in the car, before I heard signs of scraping feet. He was hiding on the other side of the car.

I jumped up onto the roof and saw the man who I had caught with a baseball bat to the face the first time. Without hesitation, I dispatched him as well.

The scene was a mess. It wasn't what I hoped for. I'd hoped to go in quietly, for people not to see me and leave them all unconscious and with explanations that didn't seem to fit.

Instead, I'd have to make sure that the drugs were found at Randazzo's, so he took the blame for these killings, too. I ran quickly back into the house, aware that the sirens would come soon. Neighbors wouldn't come out on the street. Not when gunshots were fired. They'd stay inside.

I grabbed the two suitcases, ran out of the house and round to my bike. The briefcases I carefully tied onto the back, before jumping onboard and tearing off. Driving down alleys, away from that scene. The sirens were now audible, blaring through the night. I stopped some distance away, in a dark alley out of sight, picked up the phone and called Eamon O'Rourke.

"It's already out there, Jac," he said on receiving the call. "They're already wondering who it is."

"Get a word out. Get a word out that somebody's just seen one of Randazzo's men. I'm about five minutes from dropping this stuff off."

Randazzo ran a bookmaker in what was essentially a genuine operation. However, it was known to Eamon that the back room could store various items. It was a way to keep it away from the cops. Randazzo was good at moving things around. Since the cops thought the items were coming to one place, they'd raid it, but everything was temporarily elsewhere. If you had people on the force in your pocket, it made it a lot easier to know when the raids were coming. Randazzo's influence was massive, which is why I had to keep my own contacts very slender.

There was a light on in the bookmaker's, but it was barely visible. I could just see the chink of brightness at the bottom of the door. Eamon had said there would be a shipment that night moving. One of his friends was going to do it, some cash that needed to be laundered, but they wouldn't be getting there for another hour.

I left the motorbike in an alley two blocks away, walked round, and approached the door with the two suitcases, tapping on it. I used the rear entrance to make sure nobody could see me. The door was opened by a man slightly smaller than me. He never saw me, only the foot connecting with his jaw.

I pushed on into the room, closing the door behind me with my foot. I dumped the two cases up onto a table. The room had one at the center, three chairs lazily splashed around it. There was a sink, a coffee pot, and many papers sitting here, there, and everywhere. It was a bit of a mess, but it would do for my purposes.

I hauled the man off the floor, slapped him down, and tied a gag on him to make sure he couldn't raise the alarm. He was tied up because I needed him to be there. I needed him to be around when Donovan's men got here.

I phoned Eamon O'Rourke, advising him that the plot was underway, and to get the word to Donovan's men. I then sat down in the corner as the man watched me. He wouldn't be alive by the end of the night, as Donovan's men would come and exert their vengeance. It was the one bit that I hoped would go to plan. The one bit that wasn't in my hands.

I could kill him now, but that would look suspicious. If they came in and he was blurting out it was Jac Moonshine, they would not believe him. After all, he had the drugs and the money. He ran a safe drop for Randazzo. I waited ten minutes, and then I started peering out of the windows at the front. It was another fifteen minutes before I saw a car, and then another one.

Returning to the back room, I heard a thump on the door. Someone demanded that the place be opened. Quickly, I cut the bonds of the man in the back room, smacked him hard across the face, stunning him, before I tore off into the front bookmaker's office. I bent down and hid behind the far-off corner counter as I heard the doors being smashed in.

It took maybe two minutes. I heard his protestations. Jac Moonshine this, Jac Moonshine that. Two shots. Then another two. Then more. Then someone saying they needed to go, that they had the gear. I waited two minutes after they left before leaving by the back door.

Back at the hideout, Deck barely lifted his head as I rode the bike down into the cellar.

"Did it go well?" Deck asked. He did not know what I was doing. He wasn't privy to that sort of information, but he wasn't blind.

"Very good, Deck. All went very well. I'll make sure those biscuits are sorted for you." Right there and then, I phoned Eamon O'Rourke and told him about the biscuits.

"Biscuits?" he said. "You're coming at me with biscuits."

"It's important," I said. "One of my people needs the right sort of biscuits. You don't get to ask about it. You just get to deliver it."

"Okay," he said, "The word I'm getting is Donovan's pissed. Randazzo's getting the blame. Maybe he can send him some biscuits, too."

When I got back to my house that night, I reckoned I wouldn't get a visit from Randazzo the next day. In fact, it was four days. Those were four of the bloodiest days the city had seen in a while. In fairness, those that died were in the gangs. Donovan exacted revenge. Randazzo extracted it back. A lot of Randazzo's men went down, but it gave me four days of peace as I sat and sipped my wine, looking at the front window, at Randazzo's man watching the house.

Randazzo didn't trust me, and he was right not to, but for

him, it was a case of a woman that couldn't look after a girl. Four days I went without seeing him, and I have to say that was hell. I wanted to see what I'd done in his eyes. I wanted to see the pain, the anger. That's the only thing I missed.

Chapter 16

I kept going with the new base in the derelict house, but one thing that I didn't have was a lot of weaponry. Everything had been a one-person operation, therefore the hits were small. Taking the drugs off Donovan's man was probably one of my bigger operations, albeit with a disguise element which required a minimal level of weaponry, but there'd be more to come. I'd be happy to cause havoc and chaos, but to do that, I would need serious weaponry.

This would come from military or ex-military sources, and I'd also need to know how to use it. Jorge had taught me how to handle a gun well, but larger weaponry brought further training problems. I was better with my martial arts because I'd had so many years of training.

One thing I didn't do at this point and one thing I eternally regret was that I didn't pay enough attention to Kelly. I wasn't there for her, so caught up in my world, my vengeance, I didn't notice that I had an eighteen-year-old who was about to take the world on her own. Yet she was looking for help. Randazzo scared her. The man had basically threatened her life, and what had her mom done? Wrapped her arms around the man, let herself be owned by the man. Of course, it was all a persona, but I couldn't tell Kelly what I was doing in case she blabbed about it, in case somebody knew.

She was returning later at night though. I figured it couldn't have been that bad because every time she went out, the man watching us would go with her. I'd seen that during the day, and I had no reason to believe at night would be any different. Sometimes Kelly would get in after me. A few times I'd been out scouting for raids I wanted to do, and I'd crawl in at two in the morning and Kelly wasn't in her bed. I'd send her a text. After all, I was a worried mom, so why wouldn't I? She'd return maybe an hour later. Sometimes she'd been drinking, but not a lot. She always seemed to be okay, physically well.

When I asked her where she was, she said someone's house. She was going into some clubs as well. She wasn't old enough for some of them, but the thing about Kelly was she could turn it on. She could look like a woman in her mid-twenties when dolled up. This happened more and more often, and she started coming back later and later.

The morning she walked back in at six, I decided I needed to find out what was going on. Jac would be no good for this. This needed to come from Debbie, and then if I got followed, it would only be Debbie looking out for her girl. That's what Randazzo had told me to do—make sure she didn't get into trouble. I should have feared for our safety, but I wasn't. I was so obsessed with revenge; I didn't care what was going on.

I saw Kelly that night wearing a skirt that disappeared well up her thighs and a top that left little to the imagination. Thankfully, she'd thrown on a jacket with it, but she'd been working on her hair for at least an hour before she went out. Her boots were halfway up her thighs as well.

If I was dressing for Alan on one of those date nights as we used to call it, yes, I wouldn't have minded being dressed like that, but I wasn't eighteen and I had a man I could trust, at least I used to. Kelly was an eighteen-year-old girl going to who knew where, so she needed to be followed.

She didn't tell me she was off. I just heard the door close. Dressed in a pair of slacks and a jumper, I wasn't ready for the nightlife, but I grabbed my coat and followed her out in the door.

The subway stop wasn't far from where we lived, towards the end of the line. We were in one of the posh districts, and the subway came above ground here. Watching her get to the end of the street, I followed her, aware that a car had already joined the watchers of Kelly. When we reached the subway, I sat some distance from Kelly, but I saw a man in a gray suit get a lot closer.

The journey on the subway was uneventful. Kelly was two carriages down and I could see her. The gray-suited man was in the same carriage as she was and occasionally, he would glance over to see what she was doing. She was on her phone messaging someone. She, like all of her age, was always on her phone.

Kelly got off the subway downtown, close to where all the nightclubs were. It wasn't a posh end of the town. There were a lot of bars and a lot of places a girl like her could get into trouble. Hopefully, she was meeting a man. Hopefully, this was well established. I wouldn't mind, as long as he wasn't some ridiculous age. If he was just a boy and he seemed to have his wits about him, I probably wouldn't even interrupt her.

Kelly took me on a wild goose chase, hopping from one bar to another. Time and again, I got some strange looks. I wasn't dressed for a night out on the town. I looked like I would be more at home at a Tupperware party. At one point, a couple of guys even tried to muscle in on me, but I gave them an abrupt shift.

After going through a couple of clubs and seeing Kelly talk to some young girls, she went into a nightclub. I really wasn't dressed for a nightclub. I would've stuck out like a sore thumb, and the bouncers probably would've either turned me away or asked me who I was looking for and gone and got the underage girl back out. That wouldn't suit my purposes.

I wanted to meet this person she was dressed up for. So far, everyone she'd met was a woman, a young girl really, most of them less than twenty-five, but now I wondered if she'd meet anyone inside. I paced around the street, monitoring the entrance. The gray-suited man had followed us. He hadn't seen me, but he'd been in several of the bars. I saw him watch her go into the nightclub and then he disappeared. I recognized it as one of Randazzo's establishments, albeit one on the legitimate side of the business.

It rained, so I pulled up the collar of my coat. I needed to know what she was up to, who she was up to it with. The time got to half-past one in the morning, and I thought about going into the club. Sure, they'd kick out soon, wouldn't they? I saw the door open, and Kelly came out, dressed for a downpour. The rain was about to increase, for I could feel the freshening breeze coming down the street.

There were several nightclub goers now milling about, some looking for taxis, but behind Kelly was walking a man. I didn't see his face at first because he was on the other side of her, and together they started strolling down the street. The rain erupted, and I saw them go to an alleyway. Were they taking shelter or were they up to something else? *Well, not until I knew who he was.* I danced across the street, avoiding several of the cars, and walked down the alley behind the pair of them.

"Kelly," I shouted.

She turned around, and we stood in the light of a small lamp over a rear door. I could see the shock on her face, almost anger. I continued towards her and then the man stood in the lamplight with her, his arm around her. It was Eamon O-bloody-Rourke. What in the name of hell? How did she get with Eamon O'Rourke? I almost lost it then, but I didn't. I stayed composed even though underneath, my blood was boiling.

"Who the hell's this?" I asked.

"Did you follow me? Did you bloody well follow me?"

"Of course, I bloody followed you, stupid girl. You-Know-Who was around, You-Know-Who threatened you."

"You can say it in front of Eamon. Eamon knows. Eamon's protecting me."

"Eamon's protecting you. How the hell is he going to protect you from Randazzo?" I raged.

Eamon went to step in front of Kelly. "Now, now, I can look aft . . ."

"You shut up," I said to him. "This is a mother-to-daughter thing. I don't give a toss who you are. You shut up."

"Eamon knows about Randazzo. Eamon knows how he works. Eamon's keeping me safe."

"Oh, yeah?" I said. "But for what price?"

I caught her hand as she went to slap me. "Is that what you think of me? You seriously think that's what I do? I'm not like you. You let him put his hands all around you. You let him roam all over you. I'm no whore."

This time, I slapped her across the face. Eamon went to step in again.

"Don't," I said, and then I turned to Kelly. "Don't you ever call me that. I sweated for you and your father, and now I am protecting you. Now I am keeping him away from you. He would've killed you. Do you get that? Instead, what are you doing? Running around out here. That's his damn club. Don't you realize? That's Randazzo's club. He'll see you. He'll watch you in there. And the guy at the front of the house, he followed you here."

"Nobody followed me here," said Kelly.

"Well, I did, and so did the guy in the gray coat who sits in the car halfway up our road. Our house is still watched. They don't come in as much. Randazzo doesn't come about, but you know what? He still watches."

I could see her anger, and just at that moment, the rain poured down. Eamon took his jacket off and put it around Kelly.

"Very chivalrous," I said.

Almost in defiance, Kelly turned and allowed Eamon to kiss her in front of me.

"Enough. I am speaking to my daughter. Kelly, snap out of it."

She turned and grabbed Eamon's hand. "You can tell me anything. Eamon and I are together now."

Inside, I was seething.

"We need a word," I said. "Eamon, can you go to the end of the alley, please? Just keep an eye out for us while we have a word."

Eamon turned to look at Kelly, but I put my hand up in front of his face. "Hello, the adult spoke here—off you go."

Eamon looked agitated. He went to reach inside a pocket.

"Don't lift out a knife," I said to him, "Because you'll not see my daughter ever again. I don't come down to places like here if I can't handle myself. Kelly will tell you. I can deliver a beating."

Eamon looked at Kelly, who nodded. It was the first time I saw Kelly's defiance fall, almost as if she was worried the situation could go badly. As he walked away, she hung her head.

"Look, Kelly," I said, "I get it, I really do. I haven't been about for you. It's just tough. Your father's dead and I've got no one to go to, no one for, well, this sort of comfort that you're getting. I've got someone who's leching all over me, a guy so powerful that it's difficult to keep him away from you and yet he is also coming after you. He was ready to kill you and I've got to keep him appeased, but Kelly," I said, lifting her head up, "he ain't been anywhere that your dad's been. He isn't in his place. Until I can get us out of here, until I can get us to a better place, I've got to keep playing along. You get that, don't you? I'm playing along. I'm trying to keep you safe."

"I want him gone, Mom," she said. "I want him gone. I don't feel safe. Eamon's keeping me safe."

"Do you know how tough Eamon is? If Randazzo came, could he protect you?"

"Can you?" quipped Kelly. "Eamon's wise about what goes on. I know that's Randazzo's club, but I don't cause any trouble. I just want some fun. Eamon shows me fun."

"Are you?"

"You're not asking me that," she said.

I thought for a moment. I probably didn't even want to know the answer. "Just be careful," I said to her. "Be careful because he may think he knows Randazzo and his people and how to handle him, but he's evil. Randazzo is a piece of work, and he will not hesitate to kill you or Eamon or me. He killed your father. He killed your father and then stood at his funeral. He came in after his funeral and tried to get intimate with me, the widow. These are not good people, Kelly. We need to get away when we can. Don't put down too many ties."

"Oh, Eamon will come with us."

"Don't put down too many ties."

I stepped forward and hugged my girl. It was about as close as we'd got since Alan died, but then I heard her suddenly scream. I broke off and turned, looking back up the alley. There was a car there and Eamon was being dragged into it by several large men.

"Eamon," shouted Kelly, and started running up the street on her heels, clipping ungainly away. I was in rather more comfortable footwear and raced up to be told by someone to keep out of it. Kelly arrived on my shoulder just as the car doors were closed and a face looked through the window at us. It was almost snarling.

"That's Randazzo's man," said Kelly. "Randazzo's men have got him. Why have they got him?"

She was in tears, distressed. *Why had they got him?* To Kelly, I was worried about Eamon, worried about her. She didn't know about the other side of Eamon, that they can find some way leading to Jac Moonshine? I needed to know. I couldn't risk Eamon telling anyone anything.

Chapter 17

I needed to get hold of Eamon, to find out where he'd gone, to find out who had him and what they were doing with him. The biggest worry I had was he would talk about Jac Moonshine. Eamon had never seen Debbie as Jac, but Deck had. If they could hunt back to the base, they could find Deck. Maybe they could torture him into saying who I was. Of course, Deck didn't know my name, but he could draw a picture.

Debbie had another problem. I had Kelly on my arm, crying her eyes out about Eamon, panicking. I couldn't go straight after Eamon. I couldn't hunt down that car. I was also out dressed as a mom. I needed to think quickly.

"Kelly? Kelly, listen to me. I'm not happy about this. I'm not sure where it's safe. I'm going to call a friend and put you up in a hotel for the night. They may have come for Eamon, but they may also come for you. I think the safest thing to do is to put you somewhere else."

"Well, what about Eamon? We should go to the police."

"If Randazzo's got him, the police will not get him back. I might find out a bit of information if I talk to Randazzo."

"No," snorted Kelly, "you can't. You know how he feels about you. You know what he'll try. You can't."

"Kelly, you're eighteen. It's time to let Mom be Mom. It's time to let me do what I do. I need to protect you."

I called up a cousin of Alan's. It was after two o'clock in the morning, and when he picked up the phone, he knew it was serious.

"David," I said, "I wouldn't call you at this hour, but I need help."

David was an accountant like Alan, and he'd warned Alan several times about going with Randazzo. A loveable rogue, David was also a good guy.

"I'm worried, David. I'm worried about Kelly. Her boyfriend's just got lifted by Randazzo. I want to put Kelly in a hotel and I want you to stay with her. I need to get back to the house in case Randazzo comes round. I can always say Kelly's staying with friends."

"Debbie, come too. We could get you out. Get you away somewhere."

"Now's not the time, David. I need you to do this for me. Will you do it?"

"Of course I will," he said. "I'll book into a hotel. Willoughby Lodge on the east side of town. I'll go there. It won't be a problem as I've used them before. Be there in about an hour."

I took hold of Kelly and walked her several streets away before stopping inside a café bar that was still open. We headed into the far recesses of it and I pumped her full of tea until it came time to jump outside and grab a cab. The Willoughby was quiet as it was after three when I dropped Kelly off. David, a short man, but with a generous smile, opened the door to his room and gave Kelly a smile. She knew him from family gatherings, and he showed her a bed to lie down on.

"Don't worry, Debbie. I'll look after her. Just be careful. Going to Randazzo is a dangerous game."

"I know," I said, "but it's something I need to do. I may be a while doing it though. I can't exactly summon him."

"Whatever it takes. We'll hole up here. I'll get Sandra to cover if need be." Sandra was David's wife.

When I got back into the taxi, an enormous sense of relief swept over me. I was about to go into Randazzo's organization. Out of nowhere, they were holding Eamon. It was going to be a case of grabbing hold of some of Randazzo's men and follow the leads. Someone would know. Someone would. Bit by bit, I was going to have to track down where Eamon had gone. Jac was relishing the task.

I got the cab to drop me about six blocks away from my new base. As I entered, Deck looked up at me from behind a bottle he was supping on.

"Funny time of the morning."

"Funny circumstances. I need to warn you, Deck, we may have a breach in our confidentiality. People may come here."

"What are they going to do with a bum like me? I'll keep an eye, don't worry. I'm able to blend away into the background."

He was, too. All he wanted was the food and drugs brought to him. If I didn't get Eamon back, I was going to have to do that myself. Maybe the base would be a good place for Eamon to hang out once I got him.

By the time I had changed and taken out the motorbike, it was five in the morning and there was only an hour before daylight would filter in again. There was a man near the docks who seemed to have a way into Randazzo's organization. Eamon had spoken about him several times and I'd seen him on a couple of the less violent escapades against Randazzo. He ran several boats that Randazzo's men would use to route via the major river into the city. Maybe he would understand what was happening.

I cruised down to the dockside. Jumping off the bike, I traipsed across several streets before spying the little shack that Eugene occupied. He had plenty of cameras around it, and I knew that inside, a barrage of screens told the tale of the outside. He could run, as he was on the waterside and close to a boat. I thought I would use this to my advantage.

I walked in front of the cameras and stood looking up at them for approximately thirty seconds in my Jac Moonshine outfit. There was a light on at the top of the shack, so he must've been up. After I counted to twenty, I legged it around the side of the shack and dropped into one of the boats below. They were river boats with motors and could carry about six people. They were sleek, but if you stayed down low enough, nobody would see you until they got into the boat. It was less than thirty seconds after I'd concealed myself that I saw Eugene's feet.

"It's good to see you," I said.

Eugene spun round. I saw him reach for a gun, but I kicked him in the chest. He fell backwards, sprawling on the deck, and I placed a boot to his neck while I reached down, took out his gun, and threw it into the water.

"I said, 'It's good to see you. Bit of action tonight.'"

"I know nothing."

"You know everything, Eugene," I said. He was of average size, maybe a little under five-ten, with broad shoulders, but he had a large, rounded belly. He didn't rely on his own strength to keep them safe. He relied instead on his charm and intelligence network, and failing that, the gun he carried in his pocket. Well, that was gone. Let's see if his mouth could still operate.

"Somebody went missing tonight, spirited away by Randazzo's men. Someone identified one of them. What's going on?"

"I told you I know nothing."

I lifted my foot, stomped down hard on him. "Does that bring back any memories?"

"I know nothing."

"Has Randazzo sanctioned anything?" There was a shake of the head. "It's somebody else. You know he's gone missing, don't you?"

He looked up at me. Eugene's eyes were not good at concealing things, but he knew.

"Somebody wants Eamon O'Rourke," I said. "Somebody must be trying to impress Randazzo. If Randazzo didn't sanction it, then they're getting at who? Eamon O'Rourke was rescued by me. Is this a go at me? Is this trying to bring in someone who's attached to me, or is it more?"

"Nothing to do with you. It's not you. Just let it be. It's Randazzo's personal business."

I stamped the hard heel of my shoe into his stomach again. "It's my business," I said. "Whose business is it?"

"It's Randazzo's. Just let it be, please," Eugene was pleading, but it was insincere. This time, I really brought my foot down on his stomach. He doubled up and vomited.

"Like I said, I need to know what this is about. If it's not about me, who is it about? Why Eamon O'Rourke? Who's got him?"

"You didn't hear it from me."

"Well, that'll be up to you," I said. "If what you tell me is true, I won't be back. Randazzo might visit. You'll have to explain to him where I found the information, but I'm sure you can cope with that. Either that or you'll jump on one of these boats and keep going. It's a big ocean out there. But whatever, who is it?" I pressed down with my boot, but not that far in yet. I gave him a chance to speak.

"Lodi," he said, "Randazzo's number three. It's Lodi. He's got him. I ran them to the dock, a warehouse at the back. That's as good as me gone then."

"Not really," I said. "Tell me how many are involved; tell me who they are. They won't be speaking after tonight if you tell me everything."

It was important to me that Eamon O'Rourke could still walk about. If Lodi had only worked this through Eugene and nobody else knew, except for the cronies with him, I could shut down the information exchange. Eugene would tell nobody that he'd given away people within the organization. Randazzo would come around and put a bullet in his head. Even if it was nothing to do with Randazzo.

"Three of them, three of them took him. Lodi, Mason, Jock. Lodi is number three for Randazzo. He wants to get up above Eddie Tumbler. Tumbler's under a lot of pressure. Randazzo's told him he wants you brought in; wants to know who you are. Eddie Tumbler's been kicking about, making noises, but he's got nowhere. Lodi thinks that Eamon's working for you. That's why he was rescued by you that night."

"He was rescued by me that night, because somebody needed to tell Randazzo what I'd done. Nobody works for me except me. People tell me things when I talk to them."

"That's all I know," said Eugene. "Please, if you go, make sure you finish them all."

I took my foot off Eugene's belly, skipped up the steps onto the dockside, and looked down at the man lying beside his own vomit. He was clearly struggling. I ran off to find my motorbike and then rode up the dockside to the warehouse that Eugene had indicated. It was one that was in use during the day. Maybe Randazzo ran it. It had large wide doors, but it looked like they had small offices high in the building.

Daylight was peeking above the horizon. Give another hour or two, and people would turn up for work. The docks would be alive.

I parked the bike not far away. I didn't want to run too far for it in case things went wrong. The gate into the warehouse compound was lying slightly open, looking like it had been broken before. I worked my way inside, following the shadows into the warehouse building.

Maybe there were cameras inside because I couldn't see any on the outside. Slowly, I approached the warehouse door, ignored it and instead opened a fire exit. Stepping inside, I could see boxes everywhere, loads ready to be packed on pallets in the morning, and a small set of metal steps that went up to a high office. There was only one way in, one way out, but there was a light on up there. I could hear some violence; the odd punch being thrown. Somebody was shouting at Eamon, using his name along with expletives and various names.

I crept over to the stairs. I ducked back into the shadows as someone stepped out of the office door. He was holding a machine gun of some sort, looking this way and that. He stepped back inside. The shot wasn't that far, and I reckoned I could handle it.

I waited for him to come back out again. I heard the door open, and he completed two steps. My silenced weapon fired, and it hit the man in the head, causing him to tip forward. His gun hit the steps with a clunk, but I was already on my way up. The second bullet hit him in the head as well. I drew level with the office, and saw inside another goon, shooting him through the window.

I couldn't see anyone else, because the middle window was obscured, but instead of running in through the door, I jumped onto the handrail and then up onto the roof. I stood waiting and sure enough, someone else stepped out, gun waving.

I dropped behind them, driving an elbow into the back of their head as I came down. I then smacked their head off the side, causing their gun to fall down before hauling them inside the office. Eamon O'Rourke was sitting in the corner on a chair, bloodied and battered. He probably had some teeth missing as well. He was cut and bleeding here, there, and everywhere.

I hauled the man currently in my arms in front of him, his neck held in a vice-like grip. I pulled down Eamon's gag.

"Who am I holding?" I asked Eamon.

"That's Lodi. The guy that went outside was Jock. Mason's on the floor." I looked down and saw the man twitching. He was nearing death.

"Has anyone else been with you tonight?" I asked Eamon.

"Eugene, down the docks, brought us over on the boat."

"I've spoken to Eugene. He advised me I should kill these people. That way, no one will know you've been here."

Eamon spat out some blood. "That's a good call."

I wrapped my other arm around Lodi's neck and quickly snapped it. He fell to the floor, and I undid Eamon's bonds. A quick shot to the temple of Jock made sure he moved no more, but Eamon had to rest on me as we clambered down to the warehouse floor.

"They hit my knees with a hammer. I can barely stand," he

said. "I think I might've lost some blood."

"Until we know you're in the clear, I'm taking you elsewhere. We'll go back to the hideout. Deck can look after you up top."

Eamon shook his head. "No, I need to check on Kelly. Make sure she's all right." I nearly told him she was, but then I checked myself. "Who?"

"The girl I was with tonight. Need to make sure she's okay. Her mother's heavily into Randazzo."

"Where does she live? What's the address? I'll check it for you."

"I'd rather do it myself." I stopped and turned to him.

"You work for me. You want to do it yourself? You walk to that door. You'll be dead before you get out of here. You're alive for now because I need you. You continue to do well for me, and we're all good. You run around with talk like this and start causing me hassle, and I'll end you."

As the sun came up, I rode the motorbike inside the safe house, down into the cellar, with Eamon hanging at the rear. I then helped him clamber up a couple of floors to the top of the building. It took a while to clean up, but I brought him bandages and food and I told him not to go anywhere until I said it was clear.

I left Kelly at the hotel. She'd be okay in David's protection. I went home, took a shower, and I went to bed. I was exhausted. I realized just how close Kelly was to being involved in all this. I needed to talk to her properly. Things were not good.

Chapter 18

One of the annoying things about young people is that they don't listen. I know I sound like a whiney mom when I say that, but they don't; they think they know best. I'm not talking about Kelly. I'm talking about Eamon O'Rourke. To me, he's young even though he is in his early twenties. The thing is, he hasn't been staying in at the safe house. Instead, he's been going out and meeting Kelly.

I let her come back to the house twenty-four hours after I had disposed of Lodi and his men. I just said disposed, didn't I? That's the thing. It had become like garbage collection; I just took out the trash. It was a horrible thing to say about anyone, any human being, but that's where my mind was. These people were trash.

I guess it makes it easier. I guess that's why I can pull that trigger and not worry about them. By this stage, I wasn't worried. But do you remember when I hit that first security guard and I felt sick to the core? I think if I hit any innocent bystander now, I would feel the same. But Randazzo's men, Donovan's men, Kozlov's men—all irrelevant.

As I was saying, Kelly was going out to see Eamon because the stupid guy hadn't stayed put. I was pretty sure after a day that Kelly was safe enough. If Randazzo had had an issue with her, he'd have been round, but Kelly had done nothing. She was at the club. The boy she was with got jumped.

The other thing I noticed, after having a little excitement, if you can call hunting down three of Randazzo's men and killing them excitement, is that life swings back to normal quickly. Randazzo came round, did his usual thing with me, missing out Kelly, and I got the stares from her again. It was disappointing after she had cried on my shoulder, after she had turned to her mother. But then that's why they're teenagers, isn't it?

I was ironing about three or four days later and down came Kelly. I could tell she was in a foul mood because she had that scowl. Normally, I don't talk to her when she has that scowl because there's nothing good coming my way, but I was still worried about her.

"You okay?"

"Of course, I'm not okay. Why did I have to be born here?"

"What the heck's that supposed to mean?"

"Why was I born here? I was talking to Eamon."

My first thought, of course, was, "How the hell have you been talking to Eamon?" but I couldn't say that. "Oh, somebody rescued him then?"

"Jac Moonshine got him back. Why can't you be more like Jac Moonshine? Look at you, standing, ironing. That outfit there, you don't wear that one normally. That's just a top for when Randazzo comes around."

"You know I need to keep him sweet. I have to keep him at arm's length. You don't do that by shunning him. He's not a man that will take that."

"He's not a man who's going to stay at arm's length for a

while, anyway. Eventually, he'll want . . . well, he'll want you."

"We'll be out of here by then. Something will change; you'll see." I focused on my ironing, hoping that would be the end of the conversation, but no such luck.

"Eamon was talking about Da. He said he wasn't any good. Randazzo's front man said Da knew all about the illegal activity."

"Your Da didn't know all about the illegal activity. Your dad definitely did not know; that was the whole point. He was running the finances of the legitimate part of the business so he could stand up in court and talk about them. The guy who covered off the other side, whoever he was, he was the one who knew about all the bad stuff. Your Da didn't."

"No, but Da knew. Da was crooked. Probably deserved what he got."

"You shut that mouth. You do not say that about your father. Your father deserved nothing of what he got. Your father worked his backside off to get you everything that you've got. You don't know what you're talking about."

Kelly gave me that look again. "No, but Eamon does. Eamon said Da knew. Eamon said he'd met a guy called Kozlov. He said that Kozlov didn't get on with Da. Da had said something."

"No. Listen, Kelly, your Da said nothing. He said absolutely nothing. He just gave a smile in the wrong place."

"How do you know that?" she said and stood there with a hand on her hip, defying me to tell her.

"Because I talked to someone, someone whose name I can't say."

"Can't say. Eamon tells me everything—tells me all their names."

In my head, I felt I needed to take Eamon to one side. The

last thing Kelly needed was names, anything the police could look to get from her. That could get her a bullet, even if she wasn't going to talk. If Randazzo knew the names she knew, she'd be a liability. If Kelly had any sense, she'd have told him to shut up, but she didn't.

Well, not in that way. These are the things that you hone over time. These are the things that experience teaches you. You can be as clever as you want, but without the experience to match it, you're just another stupid dummy. I was there at the start as well.

"You're best not knowing these things," I said. "You're best just getting on until I can get us clear, and we'll get out. We'll go somewhere nearby first, then we'll go back to Ireland."

"Why can't we go now? Why can't we?"

"Because we're being watched."

"No, we aren't. We're not being watched much. It's not like it was before. They were there all the time. Even Randazzo doesn't visit you that often. Used to be every day. Now it's down to less than every two."

"Just listen to me, Kelly. Bottle it up; keep it away from everything else and just bide your time and we will run, but we must do it when the time is right. Randazzo finds us running, and well, we'll end up like your father."

I put my head down to my ironing again, letting the warm metal slip back and forward, smoothing the clothes with a little steam. But she wasn't for moving, not one bit.

"I wish you were more like Jac Moonshine."

I lifted my eyes to look at her. It was a genuine statement. She wasn't baiting me.

"I wish you were more like him. Dad was crooked, but somebody should take Randazzo down. Somebody should end him. That Jac Moonshine, he's got guts. He just marches in, kills them, shows them what for."

"How am I going to be like Jac Moonshine?" I said. "I'm doing what I can. I use what I can. I don't like it; it's not fair."

"Maybe I can get in contact with Jac Moonshine. Maybe Eamon might know. Maybe Eamon could put me his way."

"You do not get further involved in this. You nearly lost Eamon, but Jac Moonshine turned up. You just keep your mouth shut and head down until we can get away."

Kelly walked over to the window. "See, they hardly watch us at all now. We should go. Oh, hang on," she said, "Looks like your favorite man's coming."

I instinctively touched up my hair, nestled down into my clothes, much more ready to make a show for Randazzo, and heard Kelly's tut. I told her if she didn't want to be about, she should get upstairs.

The doorbell rang. When I walked over to it to open it, it was almost as if he pushed his way in. I had barely turned the latch, and the door was flying open.

"Does your daughter know who she's messing about with?"

"Of course, she doesn't."

"I got word that she was out the other night when a couple of my guys got whacked. I want to see if she knows anything?"

"She knows nothing. Why would she know anything?"

"She was at the nightclub and then the guy she was with . . ."

"The guy she was with got jumped, taken away. I know. I had her in my arms full of tears afterwards. She's an eighteen-year-old kid. She knows nothing."

He turned and grabbed my jaw, forcing his fingers in tight. "You don't tell me what she knows; she tells me what she knows, not you. Just because I got eyes on that body doesn't mean you can use that mouth."

He put his hand down and turned his back to me. I could have taken a knife and just killed him there and then. I could have ended him, but the house was being watched, and we'd have to run. We'd never be clear. They'd know who did it. When Jac Moonshine came to end him, well, nobody would know who Jac was.

"Get her," he said to me. "Be quick about it." I walked past him, and he grabbed me from behind, his hands rough on my body. "You know your place; you make sure you stay in it."

He smacked my backside as I walked over to the stairs. When I reached the top of them, I opened the door to Kelly's room.

"He wants you downstairs," I said. "Keep it cool. Tell him you know nothing. He's asking about Eamon."

"I'll tell him what I think, I will," said Kelly. I grabbed her and shoved her up against the wall.

"If you and me are to survive, you won't. You'll tell him all about Eamon being taken, but you won't tell him any names. You won't tell him anything you know. He's just a guy in the club that you got off with, understand that? We survive until we get away. Listen to your mother, Kelly. Listen to me good, because this will be the death of you if we don't sort it out."

I took her by the hand, but I could feel her shake as she came down the stairs. As we reached the bottom, Randazzo was in the living room, and he called us through.

"I hear you want to be like your mother," Randazzo said to Kelly, and he walked over to me, slipping in behind. The next thing, I felt his hand on my throat. "You want to be with a player. Eamon's not much of a player. You could do a lot better, better like your mother has." He took a deep kiss from me before he looked back at Kelly. "Tell me what happened," he said. "Tell me what happened at the nightclub."

"I went out to dance," said Kelly. "I could get in with my fake ID."

"I heard it wasn't a fake ID that got you in. I heard it was what you were wearing. Like to show a bit, cheeky at that age. Where did you meet Eamon?"

"In the club. We danced a bit in there. We made out inside and then when we came out the front, well, he got jumped. Some guys grabbed him. They were rough on him as well. I phoned Mom. I was going to go to the police, but she said no."

"That's because your mom knows what she's talking about," said Randazzo. "The guys who took Eamon were mine. Jac Moonshine did them in. At least I heard it was Jac Moonshine. There wasn't anything left, no bottle, no nothing, but they were killed. I think Eamon knows Jac Moonshine, because that's twice she's saved him, and I want to know where Eamon is."

"I met him that night," said Kelly. "What can I tell you? I didn't know he knew you. How do you think I would have reacted to that? I'd have followed him, tried to set you up."

Randazzo looked at her, staring thoughtfully, "Yes, you would have, wouldn't you? Joined forces with him, probably come after him, gone to the police. Why not? I don't like you, Kelly," said Randazzo, "but you know what, you're telling the truth this time. Take your backside up the stairs. I need a word with your mother."

I gave Kelly a nod and watched as she disappeared up the stairs. When she'd reached the top, Randazzo closed the door to the living room. He turned and slapped me across the face, hard. "I told you to sort her out. I told you that."

"She is an eighteen-year-old kid; she got off with some guy. How am I meant to stop that? If I stop her from going out, she'll just stew in here. What she needs is away from you and me. She needs to live a better life."

"Then you better make sure that she keeps it shut." He stepped up close to me, his hand going around my throat again. "You and me are going to do this properly soon. I just don't have the time, but one of these days I'm coming for you properly, you know what I mean. Alan's been in the ground long enough."

I don't know how I held my cool at that point. I was ready to tear him apart. I really was.

"I'd do it now, but I can't," he said. "I've got someone coming that needs to be taken care of. That's the trouble with Colombians; they are always like this, impatient, don't understand I've got other matters. Once he's gone, though, I think you and I are going to have a proper conversation."

I stood and watched him go, my hands tense. I was ready to strangle him, ready to rip him apart, but I also knew things needed to move, but my chance was coming. Kozlov must be here. Randazzo was looking for a Colombian.

I could take out Kozlov, then I could go for Randazzo, his wife first, then him. I'd make him feel pain, all right, but in order to get to Kozlov, I needed to know the wheres and the whens. Eamon O'Rourke had spent enough time on the sidelines.

If he was careful, he could still operate. He could still move about. I knew that when I called him, he'd try to evade it. He'd maybe even skip town, but I didn't have a way in. I couldn't walk amongst them, so I needed Eamon. I placed a phone call and sat and listened as Eamon gave me every reason he shouldn't step back out yet. I told him I'd be visiting in a couple of hours' time and if he was in that building, he wouldn't come out of it alive.

Chapter 19

I was doing the washing when the phone call came in on my other mobile. That's one of those things you don't realize; the number of devices doubles. I needed a mobile for Jac, and I needed a mobile for me, because obviously Eamon can't have my number. It has to be Jac's number. That mobile has to be kept out of sight, otherwise, Kelly gets a hold of it and, "Why have you got a new mobile phone? Where's my new mobile phone? What type is it?" Then she tries to break into it and look at what I'm doing.

Kids are funny like that. She almost disowns you in some ways as a teenager and yet wants to know everything that you're doing. At least to check you're not embarrassing them, but it's something she can't find.

I felt it vibrating in my back pocket as I pulled the washing out. I continued to pull the clothes out and turned to shout for Kelly. She wandered into the out room, looked at me and says, "You've got to be kidding."

"No, I'm not kidding. Hang these up outside."

"It's probably going to rain, though."

"Just do it."

I picked up the basket and handed it over. She turned with

a tut, marched off, but I didn't grab my phone right away. Instead, I walked to the dining room where I could see her, but she couldn't see me. The phone continued to vibrate, whoever it was remaining on the call. I guessed it's Eamon. Nobody else had this number, so it must be Eamon.

"It's Jac," I whispered into the phone.

"Eamon. I've been out and about. It's not been easy, but I know tonight they're having a meeting down at Rocks Off."

"And?"

"They should be there anytime from about nine o'clock. I believe they've got some business to do and then there's a night of entertainment planned. At least that's what they're doing for now. You know how these people are."

"Good," I said to Eamon. "Back to the safe house. Stay off the street."

"Okay. I'm just going to get some groceries. Deck's out of his fancy stuff."

Rocks Off, I thought, slipping the phone into my back pocket and seeing that Kelly's not even halfway through the washing. Rocks Off is a strip joint. It's one of those classier ones, though. Randazzo owns several of them. They're all legit, or as legit as that kind of thing can ever be.

I was never interested in that kind of thing. Alan told me about them once and I had to be inside Rocks Off twice because Randazzo told him to bring me. That's something I realized. Back when Alan was around, Randazzo had eyes for me. He would look, but I was Alan's wife. He didn't upset the apple cart; I guess as a testimony to how good an accountant my husband was.

When Kelly returned, I asked her where she was going that night.

"I don't know," she said.

"Why don't you stay over at someone's, Louise's or somebody?"

"You trying to get rid of me?" she asked.

"I could do with a night out. It's not been easy. Might go out with a few of the girls or I might go on my own somewhere where somebody's not watching me outside."

She stepped forward and gave me a hug. It caught me off guard, and I took a moment to hug her back.

"I miss him," she said to me. "I really miss him."

I could feel the tears coming to my eyes, welling up. I'd been so determined on this revenge, so hell-bent it pushed a lot of the grief aside, but I cried on Kelly's shoulder; fits and starts then full on.

That's the thing about all this. There's still that Alan-sized hole. I said before; we were each other. We owned each other and somebody took that away from me. I guess they took it away from Kelly as well. She didn't own him, and he didn't own her, but it's that other bond, that special one, child and parent. I have it with Kelly too, but I guess when you're removed from the situation, it feels stronger. But in the middle of a mess, it's hard to let everything out.

"You go have yourself a good time, Mom, whatever it is."

Kelly was safely packed off that night and I dropped her at the house where she was staying, watched her go in, saw two happy parents waving me goodbye, not knowing what they'd taken on for the night. Then I made for the safe house. I entered the safe house with a mask wrapped around my face. It was only a scarf, but it was enough.

Deck was at the bottom, as usual, sitting with his bottle.

"Where is he?" I asked.

"He's upstairs, top floor."

I slowly crept up to the second floor and heard the footsteps of Eamon coming down the stairs.

"Stay up there," I said, "or I'll kill you."

It was harsh, but it got the point across that I didn't want to be disturbed. It took me about an hour to put together a decent disguise, red hair and such an amount of makeup on that I was unrecognizable. I put a pair of glasses on as well, shaded, so my eyes couldn't be seen. As I looked in the mirror, I thought I looked convincing enough. I certainly looked nothing like Debbie Parlor.

"Eamon, I'm off to the club. Be prepared for a phone call if things go bad. I might need a lift out."

I said that the Rocks Off strip club was one of those classier establishments, and it probably was. I don't have a substantial amount of experience for comparison between these types of joints, but when I went up flashing a bit of cash to the bouncers, I was happily let in.

I sat down in a booth towards the back, scanning the room. There were several what you would call podiums and a main stage, girls gyrating away on them. I ordered a drink and sat back. A girl came up to me asking if I wanted a private dance. She couldn't have been much older than Kelly. Well, she was, if he was running a legitimate business, but she looked so young. I waved her away, told her I was just here to relax and enjoy the environment.

It was two hours before Kozlov and Randazzo entered the club. I was sitting well back from them, and they couldn't see me, but they took seats front and center, the main stage in front of them. I waited for about twenty minutes to get an idea of what was going on, but the two of them seemed to relax.

Whatever the deal, it must have been done, because their eyes were fixed forward and there were several girls that sat beside them as well. You could see Randazzo now for who he was. Oh, he liked women, certainly liked their bodies anyway. I'd understood that from his visits. For all that Kelly had annoyed him, for all that he got angry at what I didn't do or couldn't do in controlling her, he never stopped eyeing me up. At my time of life, there was a slightly sad part of me that appreciated it, but there was a mature head in there that knew how dangerous a man like that was.

I stood up and went to the bathroom, looking for the backstage area. I spotted it on the way in, came out, and then shot through a small door into the rear. I wandered in amongst several girls getting changed into different outfits. Suddenly, several of them ran out in what must have been a changeover.

I looked around, and hanging up was a large cowboy hat. I saw what I supposed was meant to be chaps and some sort of western waistcoat. You certainly wouldn't wear the outfit outside. There was a holster and a pair of pistols as well, and some boots. Racing around quickly, I grabbed them, and clutching them tight, I hid them underneath my coat as I strode back to the women's bathroom.

Five minutes later, I was inside one cubicle wearing what could only be described as party-wear—is that how they put it? If you sat on a horse in this getup, I'm afraid your backside would be sore. You'd have skin rash where there was nothing to protect. Everything except the absolute extremities was uncovered.

I'd taken a compact out and was rubbing down my face. I put my mask on, one of those western types that cowboy outlaws would've worn, like a big handkerchief almost or a scarf. I looked at myself between the hat and the mask covering up to my eyes. I was pretty sure they would struggle to know who it was.

I'd been one of those ladies in life who've never had a tattoo, thankfully, because it's a dead giveaway, and wherever it was on my body would be seen as I stepped out on that stage. The other thing I realized was there wasn't a lot of support in this clothing. Regardless, I put the rest of my clothes into a little bag I had folded up inside my jacket. It was all stowed easily if I'd need to grab it on the way out.

Walking backstage again, I wandered between the different rooms then found a rear exit, leaving my bag down towards it. I returned close to the backstage area, watching to see any girls who were about to go on. I loitered at first, then two girls went on for about a ten-minute stint. Then I heard panic from inside the changing area.

"You're on Lily. Lily, would you get on?"

Lily came racing through and was grabbed by Jac Moonshine. I hit her hard in the neck, followed by another kick that knocked her out. I opened one door of the empty changing rooms, let Lily fall in, and closed it behind me. It was almost seamless. I walked onto the stage.

One thing that you don't realize is you can't see most of the audience looking at you. This is maybe a helpful thing, but you can see the front area and I certainly could see Randazzo and Kozlov.

Music came on and then stopped quickly as somebody realized that there was now a cowgirl on stage. A hoedown began with a disco beat behind it, and I gyrated about. I like to dance, but not like this. I remember, oh maybe ten years ago, I did a dance like this for Alan. We both ended up falling about, laughing, and it was fine because it was fun.

Up here, if you were getting paid for this, you would feel cheap. I certainly felt cheap.

The lights swirled, and I danced about. I removed some of the outfit. There were a few items—but not many—I could get rid of before I would be exposed in areas I'd rather not. As long as it was bikini like, I'd be okay, but then I saw Kozlov's face. If need be, I'd take off whatever to shoot that guy, for he would not leave here alive.

The pistol on the left-hand side in the holster was a real gun, the one on the right a fake and had caps inside. I fired the fake twice. I kept my handgun deep within the holster, for it was different and if I brought the two out together, it would surely be seen as real.

I turned, and I did what I think was called a twerk, got a few cheers, and as I worked my way to the front of the stage, Randazzo stood up and popped some money just inside the G-string I was wearing. I still had the denim chaps over the top of it, although, in fairness, they covered little.

I didn't want to hang around though, and I soon maneuvered myself, dancing straight in front of Kozlov and Randazzo. I bent this way and that, desperate for the girls that were hanging onto them to move out of the way. I was an excellent shot, but with how warm I was feeling, the sweat pouring off me, music pumping in my ears, and the fact I'd be shooting with my left hand made it even more difficult a shot.

I dropped the denim chaps and let go of the cowboy waistcoat. That grabbed their attention, and I saw Kozlov step up, coming towards the stage. I didn't understand what he was saying. Maybe it was in Colombian, but he was clearly egging for me to remove more.

I stomped my right foot, stomped my left foot, took the right pistol out and fired into the air, and then pulled out the left one and fired it twice, straight between Kozlov's eyes.

He had only been five feet away. There was a momentary shock. The music was still playing, a lot of the other girls were still dancing, but then panic and horror set in. I didn't see it because I had turned and run off the stage.

I went straight down the corridor to the rear of the building, grabbed my bag, dropped a Jac Moonshine bottle of hootch, hit the fire escape door, and ran out, still in my mask. The cool air hit my skin, but I didn't stop. I ran for around three blocks before I got into my bag and threw my coat around me. I whipped the cowgirl boots off, put on my stilettos, rubbed myself down as best I could around the face, and then hailed a cab.

The direction I wanted to go would've taken me past the club, but I instead asked to go downtown. Once there, I got out and hailed another cab back up to just a few blocks from the safe house. From there, I walked back in. Once inside, I checked with Deck that Eamon was on the top floor. I took a bottle of water from the middle floor and washed myself down. Then I wrapped up all the clothing I'd run out of the club in.

I dressed back in my normal clothes, told Eamon to wait here for further instructions, and said goodbye to Deck on the way out. I reached home that night knowing I'd be alone, Randazzo wouldn't be about, and there was nobody watching the house. The man had moved to watch Kelly and her friend. I got in, changed into my pajamas, and lay in bed.

I thought I would go straight to sleep after the exertions of the evening, but I didn't. I sat and watched a video that night. It was Alan and me and I was so happy with it. Kelly had just been born, and I was holding her in my arms. Alan was there in front of our house, and then I saw him in the background, Randazzo. If I had a glass of wine, I'd have raised him a toast. His wife was next. I'd really put the cat amongst the pigeons with this one. The game was properly afoot.

Chapter 20

As I look back, it strikes me I failed to keep Kelly out of it. At the start, that was my intention. Kelly wouldn't be involved. I underestimated her reaction to her father's death. I underestimated that, like me, she would want him avenged. Kelly is a chip off the old block.

Until that point, though, Kelly's involvement had been Kelly's doing. Well, I say that, but in truth, she was involved because of Alan's work. Who Alan worked with brought her to the attention of goons like Randazzo and Eddie Tumbler, but she was the one who got involved with them by trying to kill those who had murdered her father at the club. I got that.

Maybe at eighteen, I'd have done that. Maybe I'd have done it at twenty-five, but I was older now. I knew the danger these people posed. I knew you couldn't trust your own emotions. I had a bit of training behind me, and I knew how to blend into the background, how to play somebody else while achieving my aims.

I guess that doesn't come easy to a teen. They get told they can change the world, or they get told they can do nothing. Nobody ever sits down and says, "Do you know what? You're going to have to be subtle about this. You're going to have to plan this out. You could be devious, or you might have to be someone else for a bit, please certain people, and then once you've got the part nailed, you can hit on exactly what you want to do. Call your own shots, be who you really are."

But Kelly was really brought into the fray by me. I lost it.

It wasn't long after I had killed Kozlov, maybe three days. I remember Kelly had said she was tired. She'd given me another hug. We'd had a couple of those in the previous few days. She seemed to be coming round to the idea that Mom might be able to help her.

Eamon was off limits because he had disappeared, stuck in the safe house by me. In fairness, she needed someone, and she didn't have that many people she could trust. She was feeling lousy, quite down, and I had told her to have a bath. She disappeared upstairs, and the other phone vibrated in my back pocket.

"It's Jac."

"Eamon here. I was out today briefly. There's a bounty on your head."

"A bounty?"

"Yes, not far off a million."

The least they could do was round it up. "You think it'll have much effect?"

"Unsure. None of the ordinary guys are going to want to go for it. After all, you went inside one of Randazzo's places and took out his supplier right in front of his face. He's probably wondering why you didn't take him out at that point as well."

"What do you think he's thinking?" I asked.

"That you aren't done, that you'll be coming for more. You're not just satisfied with killing him. From what I've heard, though, he's panicking because he doesn't know why you're doing it."

"Too many bodies in the past, too many skeletons in the cupboard." I laughed down the phone. There was a ring on the doorbell.

"Sit tight, Eamon. Don't worry about the bounty; there'll be nobody left to pay it."

I closed down the call and walked to the front door. I checked through the eyepiece to see Eddie Tumbler standing outside. Slowly, I opened the door.

"I'm wanting a good-looking lady," said Eddie, and hustled his way into the house. The way he said it scared me. They could be like that, and I'd seen them operate with other women. I'd always had Alan's protection, and I was always glad that Randazzo so far hadn't gone down this path. But Eddie, on this occasion, seemed to be more agitated, more determined.

"Look, Eddie, I don't think that's wise. I don't think that you should, really . . . you know, you're a nice guy and all that, but Randazzo, he's got his eye on me. It wouldn't work for either of us, Eddie. He'd come for us both."

Eddie, who'd walked through my living room, was opening and looking through other doors. "I'm not coming for you. Why would I want you? Where is that daughter of yours?"

My heart sank. He couldn't be serious. Kelly, he wanted Kelly. Suddenly, it was dawning on me. He'd wanted Kelly all along. He had a thing about her. He'd thought that when Randazzo took me up as his woman on the side, then he could move in with Kelly, have her as one of his extras.

There was no idea of flattery here. Don't be mistaken. You were there to be used. You didn't get a say in where and when. You didn't get wooed. Oh yes, they'd make a scene of giving you flowers or some diamond necklace or that, but you'd have to be so cheap to accept that sort of thing.

"Are you sure that's wise?"

Eddie turned to me and put his finger in my face. "I'm not asking for your advice. I'm asking where your daughter is."

Of course, with Kozlov being shot, was Kelly in the picture? There's no way they could have thought that was Kelly on the stage. I mean, I know my daughter and I are alike, but there's a fair bit of difference in the look of a mature woman like me and a young thing like Kelly. I just called myself mature. I'd only ever do that in the defense of my daughter.

I grabbed Eddie's wrist as he walked to the hallway door. He would go upstairs next. Kelly was in the bath and that was like a red rag to a bull.

"She's not ready at the moment," I said. "She's sorting herself out."

He turned and slapped me across the face. It was hard, very hard. "Told you to keep the hell out of it," he said to me.

"Don't do this, Eddie," I said. "Please!" I begged. "Have me then. Have me! Come on, right now, right here."

I didn't mean it. Well, I did. I wanted him to focus his attention on me, but inside I was unraveling. This wasn't the plan.

There were three rather poor options on the table. I could let him go to Kelly—no, that would not happen. I could let him stay here with me if he'd accept. That was a deeply repulsive idea. I may murder people, but there are limits.

There was a third option. Kill him right here and now. But Kelly was upstairs. Or could I talk him out of this, but how? It was like the heat was up in him, or maybe he was worried that Kelly would get moved on. Maybe he worried Randazzo would come for her, think she was involved in this latest killing. After all, Jac Moonshine had done it and Jac Moonshine had rescued Kelly. Randazzo hadn't been happy. Did he think there was a link? There was, of course, just not the one he expected. What could I do?

I got in my head that if I brought Kelly downstairs, he would talk to her a bit, woo her, maybe have a quick fondle and go. I could suggest that he arrange something for later that night, so she would look better, and he could take her out properly. Then when he left, we would run. Just go.

"I'll bring her down. Don't go up. Don't go up, Eddie, let me bring her down. Please, Eddie." I was beseeching him like a crazy woman.

"Yes," he said, "bring her down. It'll be classier that way, won't it? You could explain to her. Get her ready."

There were tears coming from my eyes. I can put tears on when I want to. I learned that from my acting, but these came from inside. There was a terror inside of me at that moment. I didn't keep guns in my house. If I had, Eddie would probably be dead by now. But I went upstairs. With heavy legs, I climbed every step. I got to the bathroom and knocked on the door.

"Kelly, love."

"Yes?"

"I'm just going to come in." I opened the door to see Kelly lounging in the bath. I closed it behind me and locked it. She could tell instantly something was wrong.

"What's the problem?" she said.

"Eddie Tumbler is downstairs."

"And?" she said.

"Well, he wants something."

"Can't you chase him off?"

"No," I said. "He doesn't want me. He wants you."

Her hands instinctively went to cover herself up, repulsed at the idea and the thought of the man coming for her.

"We'll deal with it," I said. "We'll deal with it, but you'll need to come down. We'll suggest you and he get together later. Suggest that he take you somewhere, and then when he's left, we will run. We'll get the hell out of here. We won't stop."

Her face was almost white, the blood drained from it, and I didn't blame her. I really didn't blame her.

"You need to get out of the bath," I said, "and come down. Don't hang about either. Don't get changed, wear your long dressing gown. Make it look as if you're worried."

"I am worried."

"Yes, but you're going along with it. I'll tell him you're eighteen and you need to have a nicer experience than this for your first time." She almost said it wasn't, but I didn't want to know. I didn't ask. "Come down in a minute's time. I'll sort this," I said.

I trudged back down the stairs to see Eddie Tumbler at the bottom.

"Where is she?" he asked.

"She will be down in a minute. Come on into the kitchen. I'll get you a beer."

He looked longingly up the stairs as I walked past him, but he followed me. As I put the beer down beside him in the kitchen, he couldn't resist it. He pulled me close.

"Alan had a right pair, didn't he? Absolute right pair. Said that the first time I saw him, and you were there; he was a lucky bastard. Someone like yourself in the sheets. Bet you're a . . ."

"Don't," I said. "Don't. Don't have me being talked about when she walks in. I'm her mother."

He gave a snort, but not a sign of regret or apology. Kelly entered the room a minute later in her dressing gown, which caused Eddie Tumbler to get up from a chair. He walked over to her, slid behind her with his hand running across her neck.

"Oh yes," he said. "You're the right feisty one, aren't you? You really are."

"Eddie," I said, "why don't we make this classier for her? Kelly's not used to this sort of thing. Why don't we get her looking all nice and gorgeous for you? You could take her out tonight somewhere classy, and then back here or back to your place. Break her in gently."

He said nothing and continued to walk round and round, staring at her.

"How about it, Eddie?" I said. "Why don't we do that? She's got some great outfits. You'll be well pleased with her."

He stood between me and Kelly. "You might not want to stay for this," he said to me over his shoulder, and I saw him reach forward, taking Kelly's dressing gown in both hands. "Or you can stay."

I've never moved so quickly in my life. In two steps, I had picked up the large kitchen knife. Another two steps, and I had buried the blade deep in his neck. He spasmed, but I didn't linger. I wasn't some scared, reactive woman, her first time having stabbed a man. Instead, my hand went up to his head, held it tight while the knife was whipped across his throat.

I let him drop to his knees and stood listening to his last gurgles.

"Nobody touches my Kelly. Nobody!"

My hand was covered in blood, the floor drowned in red. I looked up and saw Kelly's shocked face, and yet I didn't see terror. Yes, there was horror at the situation. Yes, there was shock, but there was relief.

Chapter 21

"Mom! Mom!"

Kelly ran forward, throwing her arms around me. She stepped in the blood on the floor, then she got it on the back of her dressing gown from my hands. It was hanging half open, and she clung onto me tightly.

"Thank you," she said. "Thank you."

"Shit," I exclaimed. "Bollocks, bollocks, bollocks! We need to clean this up. Got to deal with this. There's no point worrying about what you've got on now. Keep it on. Get some cloths and towels."

Kelly went into shock again at how her mother had just started domestic duties, as if it was just another one of those bad spillages on the floor. I told her to watch her feet, and we got some tea towels, wrapping them around her feet and then mine once we were clear of the blood. That way, we could walk through the rest of the house. We picked up some sheets and another lot of towels.

It took over an hour to wipe up the blood off the floor. It was copious. We were wringing them out in the sink, praying that nobody came to the house. I wrapped the body up in the cloths, just about covering it fully. All the spare cloths had gone into the washing machine, and our clothes were about to follow. I'd pulled the blinds down at the back of the house so no one could see, and the two of us together stripped off and put all our clothing into the washing machine.

I stood at the sink while Kelly washed her hands. Once she was clean, I told her she needed to go upstairs, and I washed mine. Really, I wanted a shower, but with a body on the kitchen floor, I wasn't going anywhere until I knew I'd got it out of the house. It was as I was rinsing off and checking myself in one of the kitchen mirrors to make sure all the blood had gone that the doorbell rang. It was accompanied by a thunderous knock.

I almost froze, but instead ran quickly up the stairs, grabbing my dressing gown, and put it on before running back again. I looked outside, hoping to put off whoever was there.

It was Randazzo. No such luck. He thundered against the door again. Slowly, I opened it.

"Where's that stupid daughter of yours, huh? Where is she?"

"She's upstairs. Why?"

"I want to make sure it's not her. I want to make sure that . . ."

"Make sure she's not what?" I asked, but got a slap across my face. I was getting pissed at this rough treatment.

"I'm not asking permission," said Randazzo, and stormed up the stairs. At least he wasn't going for the kitchen. Kelly came out onto the landing at the commotion and then stood. I could see how clammy her skin was, still reeling from what had just happened. I wondered if Eddie Tumbler's car was outside. I looked from Randazzo to Kelly. He just stood there, looking at her.

"Dance," he said.

"Dance?" blurted Kelly. "What do you mean, dance?"

"Dance like you're entertaining a man."

He stared at her. Then he stepped forward, quickly opened her gown, and then shut it again. "Dammit," he said. "It wasn't her."

He turned away, leaving a rather shocked Kelly holding onto her decency. "It wasn't her what?" I asked. "You're not making any sense. Raz, tell me. You're not making any sense. What's she done?"

"Bitch Jac Moonshine came in and took out someone in front of me at a strip club, dancing away. I thought it might be your Kelly, but figures I was wrong. It's not her."

"When was this?" I asked.

"A couple of nights ago."

"She's been with me mainly, over at Louise's one night."

Randazzo turned to me. "I know that. I damn well know that. I just needed to make sure."

I reached up and stroked the back of his neck. "You're very tense. Is it . . ."

"It's that bitch again."

I had hoped that they never would realize that Jac Moonshine was a woman, but I guess the strip club incident kind of gave that away. There was no way a man could have been on stage, not wearing that little and not be mistaken. Randazzo stormed down the stairs, and I followed him.

"I need a drink," he said and started marching towards the kitchen. I hurried past him.

"Go have a seat in the living room. I'll bring one in. You want the usual, scotch?"

"Yes, yes. A large one," he said.

I raced into the kitchen, looking at the rather obvious body wrapped in cloths, lying in the middle of the floor. I jumped over it twice, getting a glass, ice, and the scotch, but I was quick about it. Returning to the living room, I sat down beside Randazzo.

"There you go," I said. "You'll get her. You'll get her. Kelly's under control now, though. You don't have to worry about Kelly. I know she went wild, but I've sorted her, Raz. I've sorted her. I mean, look what you just did up there, and she didn't react back against you."

His hand went out. He pulled me towards him by the back of my neck, planting a large kiss on me.

"I said Alan had picked a good one. He really had, hadn't he?" His finger ran down the nape of my neck and then further. I swore he was going to go further, but the doorbell rang.

"You'd better answer that," he said. I stood up thankfully and walked towards the door. Through the eyepiece, I could see it was a Detective Frogg on the other side.

"Who is it?" asked Randazzo.

"It's Frogg."

"Well, let him in," said Randazzo. "Nothing to hide here." How little he knew.

I opened the door to the rather thin and gaunt-looking Frogg. He gave me a nod and then strode into the living room. "Mr. Randazzo, I hear things got very hot at one of your strip clubs."

"We don't get the protection of the police," said Randazzo.

"Somebody told me," said Frogg, "that a certain Mr. Kozlov was shot within your club. He's a known drug dealer, Colombian."

"Who told you that?" asked Randazzo.

"I do need to protect my sources," said Frogg. "Somebody said there was a bottle left behind."

I could see the agitation on Randazzo's face. I didn't need

this. I just wanted everyone to clear out.

"Maybe you could catch the damn killer for once. Maybe you could do your bloody job."

"You've got to admire whoever's doing it, don't you? Leaving you a bottle behind with their name. That's quite something, quite clever. They must hold a serious grudge against you. Saying that, it could be anyone, any number of people. Well, it'd have to be a woman. It'd have to be someone that you really pissed off."

Frogg looked over at me, but only briefly. I felt a shudder. Did he know? Randazzo never turned his head, almost thoughtful in his drink.

"How many attacks have they managed on you now? How much money have they cost you? I guess it'll cost you big with this one. Kozlov coming to be entertained by you; ends up dead. Donovan's going to be pissed. His best supplier gone. I've got to be honest; I'm delighted. Whoever it was has done this city a heck of a favor. Although I guess you'll find another way. Business people are like that, aren't you? Roll with the punches, know what to do. But whoever she is, she's got you by the balls."

Randazzo jumped up, almost racing at Frogg. His hand went to grab him.

"I wouldn't want you to get done for assault," said Frogg. "I'll leave before I cause Mrs. Parlor here any more trouble. Good to see you, Randazzo. You look after yourself, Mrs. Parlor, and that daughter of yours, too."

Frogg went to the front door and let me close it behind him. When I came back in, Randazzo was agitated.

"I need to go."

"When will you be back?" I asked. He turned, looked at me

in my gown, bent down and kissed me. He then spent the next couple of minutes roaming around me. As he did so, my chin was resting on his shoulder, and I could see behind him towards the hallway.

Kelly appeared at the door, a large knife in her hand. I shook my head. She came closer, and again, I shook my head, putting my hands up between me and Randazzo, letting them run across his chest.

"Well, that's a first time for that," he said. "It's good to see you're understanding where our relationship's going."

Again, I gave a gentle shake of the head and my eyes flicked hard left, indicating Kelly should get out and get the knife back where it belonged.

"Take me to dinner," I said. "Take me out. Wine me, dine me, and then we can come back here."

"I've got a lot on. It'll be another three days at least before I can even think about that," said Randazzo. "I'll be here then. You make sure you're looking good."

He kissed me again and then broke off, turning around towards an empty door. Kelly had gone. I escorted Randazzo to the door, endured another couple of kisses from him, and then locked up.

"Get changed, Kelly," I said. "I'm not having any more men coming in when we're not dressed." I sat down with her then and planned what we would do.

"We won't do anything with the body until tonight. In the meantime, I will hire a car. I'll leave it close to here. We'll go out through the back tonight, so our keeper at the front doesn't notice. We won't use our car. We'll put him into the trunk of this other car, we'll take him to the docks, and I'll show you how you get rid of a body."

Kelly looked towards me, eyes suddenly raised. "Have you done this before?" she asked.

"Don't ask questions," I said. "Just listen and trust your mother."

We sat together most of the day watching some films, having dinner, and waiting for the time to tick down. It was after midnight when we took the body out to the back.

Kelly was a reasonably strong girl, but the riskiest part was going through our back gate and putting the body into the car. Fortunately, the road at the back wasn't a major street. It took us less than sixty seconds to get out and the gate closed. With the body in the trunk, I slammed it down and got us underway. I dropped by the safe house, leaving her in the car while I ran inside. She didn't ask why, and I continued to the docks. Kelly was tense at our nefarious activity, and I could hardly blame her.

Kelly wasn't a frequenter of the docks, but I showed her where the quiet places were. We left the body beside a cesspit. I'd given Tumbler a rub down to remove any of me from places I thought I had touched, and making it as sterile as possible. I left the bottle. That was what jolted Kelly. From my pocket, I took out a small bottle of hooch, left it, and she saw the words 'Jac Moonshine' on it.

"Mom, are you trying to blame it on her? Where did you get the bottle? Is this your plan, to let Jac Moonshine take the blame? Do you know her?"

"Don't ask questions," I said. "Everything's changed, Kelly. Eddie Tumbler coming on like that, Randazzo upping the ante with me. Everything's changed. Another couple of days and it will be over. Another couple of days and we'll be at a point when we'll either be running, or I'll have solved all this."

She wanted to ask. "Don't," I said. "Don't. Into the car."

She was busting to talk to me as I drove through the streets down to the poorer part of town where we had just come from. I parked two blocks away, and then walked her to the safe house.

"This place stinks," said Kelly. As we entered through the metal door, Deck jumped up, seeing me with someone else.

"Easy, Deck." I also wasn't in any makeup with Eamon upstairs. "Easy," I said. "This is my daughter. Kelly, this is Deck. Deck looks after the place for me. He's like my concierge at the desk. Is he still upstairs?"

"He's sleeping like a baby," said Deck.

Kelly gave me a shocked look, but she was clever. Inside her mind, the cogs were whirring. I walked Kelly up to the middle floor, where she could see the outfits, the makeup desk, everything that I could use to disguise as Jac Moonshine. I then took her up another flight of steps where a man was lying on a small camp bed. Kelly's face lit up.

"It's Eamon!"

She ran over, throwing her arms around him. He woke up with a fit and a start and then broke into a smile when he saw her. They kissed and held each other. Then it seemed to get a bit too personal for my liking.

"Not now," I said to the two of them. "She can't stay too long."

Eamon looked over at me. "Who the hell are you?"

"You don't recognize the voice?" I asked. "Eamon O'Rourke, you've been dating my daughter Kelly."

"You're Kelly's mom, Debbie? You're Mrs. Parlor? I saw you that night. You're the woman from that night. How are you here?"

"I saw you later that morning as well," I said. "This is an

enormous shock to Kelly as well. I'm Jac Moonshine, and we've got work to do."

Chapter 22

Mannersberg's quite a big city and one thing about large cities is somebody somewhere doesn't like you. This was no different for Randazzo, and the good people of the riverfront part of town quickly became part of my plan because of their utter hatred of the man. My overall plan changed the moment we killed Eddie Tumbler.

Originally, Eddie Tumbler would have died in front of his boss, and Randazzo's wife would have died in front of him as well. I'd have taken everything slowly while he watched. I wouldn't have touched the kids, of course, but I wanted him to know how I felt. It was one of the strangest parts of my revenge, though, because I was worried about how I would feel. After all, if they had come after me because of Alan, I would be an innocent party, a woman standing by her man. But to actively seek revenge, and on his wife?

Maybe I was wrong too. Maybe knowing that Alan was looking after the legitimate affairs of one of the nastiest men in town, I should have said not to have a word with Tumbler but instead said, "Let's go, pack up, leave, get out," as difficult as that could have been. I didn't, and his wife certainly hadn't left Randazzo knowing what he was.

After Eddie Tumbler's death, I had to step up my actions. After all, his henchman had just been taken out. The man could have imploded. Links to how Eddie saw my Kelly could be established by Randazzo, and it just felt that things were getting out of hand.

I got a hold of Eamon and told him I wanted to know where Mrs. Randazzo was going to be. I needed an opportunity, and I needed it fast. The word on the street was that Randazzo was entertaining some foreign guests up at the house. As was her custom, his wife moved out to a hotel. The kids either went with her or were sent off to some nanny. I assumed that this was Mrs. Randazzo's way of pampering herself while her man was getting up to who knew what. I guess there were a lot of women bought for him or brought in when his foreign guests were being entertained. No wife would have enjoyed that.

The hotel was called the Limelight, one of the poshest in town. It had elegant curtains; it had staff attentively waiting here, there, and everywhere in smart waistcoats and trousers. A place you didn't stay at unless you had money. There was no riffraff, and it was said that Randazzo's wife occupied a suite at the top. She, of course, had guards with her, but I reckoned I could get in.

Eamon had been good at talking to people on the street while keeping his cover low. I backed that up by entering the hotel dressed as an old woman with white hair, wandering around as if she had been misplaced by someone. The staff never questioned me, for my clothes looked expensive enough and I was polite and tipped well.

When I got up to the penthouse floor, I wandered out from the elevator towards the rooms, but was stopped by a giant of a man.

"I'm sorry, dearie," I said. "Where am I?" I could tell he wasn't used to being polite, but he held his arm out, indicating I should go back to the lift.

"This is a private floor. I'm afraid you can't come here. You'll need to go down on the lift."

"Private floor? What floor am I on? Do you know?"

He was clearly out of his depth, but he put an arm underneath mine and escorted me back to the lift. In fairness, it was probably a lot less rough than what he would do with anyone else that came up, but as I stood in the lift, he pressed the button, stepped back out and I could see at least another four people down the corridor. Mrs. Randazzo was well protected.

I waited outside the hotel for the day until late in the evening. Mrs. Randazzo appeared in some finery, helped into a car by one of her four bodyguards. There was a driver as well, which made five, plus her. I tailed the car downtown to a quiet restaurant, small and homely looking. As she was taken through without a fuss, I sat and watched the restaurant for half an hour.

No one went in, no one came out. It would be one of those places specially reserved for her. Maybe a friend would join her or maybe she's alone because she liked the food. The driver waited outside, the four bodyguards inside with her. I'd have liked to have watched this behavior several times, but it could have been another month, maybe two months, before she would be back at the hotel again. Who knew when she would come out to the restaurant again?

Time was against me. I needed to act, and yes, I was making a lot of this up on the fly. I drove back to the safe house, got changed and returned on my motorcycle, parking it in an alley across from the restaurant. This part of the city was quiet, especially as it was getting past ten o'clock, and I wondered if the street would be watched. I took out a gun with a silencer acquired for me by Eamon previously in the week. I'd have to be quick once I got inside with four goons protecting her. Carefully, I crept down an adjoining alleyway until I was at the front end of the building.

I strode quickly up to the car, grabbed the side door, but found the window being rolled down for me. The driver clearly didn't realize the threat until he saw a gun being pointed in his face. Two quick shots followed, quiet because of the silencer. I checked him once to make sure I'd connected with the head and then pushed open the restaurant's inner door.

The maître d' stood looking at me, his face going into horror. The Jac Moonshine character was becoming more of a legend, and I held a gun in his face, pushing him backwards until he opened another door behind him which led into the open restaurant. Mrs. Randazzo was sitting at a table in the far corner, a lone candle as she tucked into something that looked like spaghetti.

The goon beside her went for his weapon, but she screamed as he hit the back wall with two bullets in his head. Another stepped in from the side to be shot down immediately, and I spun to find one behind me, pulling his gun. He got close, though. Neither of us got a clean shot off, but his echoed through the night.

My gun dropped as he struck me, but I was able to step inside and across him, throwing him over my hip, taking him to the floor before driving down on his face with my knee. I grabbed my gun as the fourth man appeared from the kitchens, clearly guarding the rear entrance. I took him down while the one beneath me struggled to free himself. I drove the butt of my gun into his face before standing up and dispatching him with two quick shots. Mrs. Randazzo stood up to run, but I raised the weapon.

"Stop. We're going for a little drive," I said.

"My husband—he'll kill you for this."

"Your husband killed me a long time ago. Your husband kills many people. Maybe this time, he'll feel it." I raised my weapon over to the maître d'. "You, chairs up against that rear door. The man quickly did as instructed. "And get me some tape."

He fumbled in a drawer below his cash register, and I instructed him to tape the hands of Mrs. Randazzo behind her back, as well as several strips to keep her mouth firmly shut.

The car was still outside. I told the maître d' to lead Mrs. Randazzo to it and put her in the back. As he did so, I stepped round to the driver's side, hauled out the dead goon, leaving him on the roadside. I told the maître d' to drive the car, giving him an address to go to. It was a small warehouse down near the riverside, close to the estate that hated Randazzo. I explained to the man I'd be behind him on the bike and if there was any trouble, I would kill him through the window of the car. Clearly, Jac Moonshine had put the fear of God into everyone. He drove the car without a question.

Once inside the warehouse I had directed the maître d to, I placed a phone call to Eamon. He arrived about an hour later to find the maître d' had been knocked out cold. I had bound and blindfolded the man and told Eamon to drive him at least one hundred to one hundred and fifty miles away and gave him some cash. I had the feeling that Randazzo wouldn't take kindly to the man once he'd discovered his wife. Once Eamon had departed, I took the tape off her mouth.

She was quite an elegant woman, dressed up in clothes that

spoke of Randazzo's money, but she clearly understood the game that was afoot. Certainly more than I did, but then again, I never saw the dark side of the person Alan was working for until it was too late.

"Do you know where you are?" I asked her.

"Berlin street," she replied tersely. "You didn't blindfold me. Just taped my mouth shut. You wanted me to see it, know where I am."

"Not a happy place for your husband. You've done a lot of damage here in Berlin Street, and he owns a lot of the properties. Some people have been evicted in a very terminal way. At least that's what I've heard."

She fixated on my eyes, trying to see the person underneath, possibly to work out how to play me.

"I'm going to see what the good people of the estate think of you. You've destroyed enough lives here. At least your husband has. Maybe he'd like to see what happens to others that he loves. Vengeance, I call it. Retribution, fair and just."

"Berlin Street wouldn't have the balls," she spat. "Berlin Street is nothing. My husband will come for you," she said. "He'll come for you, and he won't kill you, not at first. He'll have his men do what they want with you. He'll humiliate you; he'll have you begging for death!"

"Humiliate me?" I railed. "He's taken all he can from me. He's taken everything. What he did to Alan Parlor."

I wasn't ready for the woman to laugh; I wasn't ready for the vile in her words. I had thought she would be like me, someone, well, not truly innocent, but someone who was kept on the sidelines, someone who didn't ask those troublesome questions. I guess it's a sin if you don't, but she clearly did.

"Alan Parlor," she said, "a weak man, who nearly ruined the

business. You realize that the Columbian connection was on a knife-edge, ready to fall apart. Alan looked at Kozlov. You don't do that, not people like that. You keep your head down. As a part of the business, he should have known that. My husband liked Alan; he ran the other parts of the business well, looked after things, made sure everything was clean.

Kozlov gave an ultimatum to my husband, wanted Parlor punished. Roberto was hesitant, but I told him business is business. We needed Kozlov's business. It took me a long time to broker that deal.

I realized she wasn't a poor wife on the sidelines; she was right in the thick of this operation.

"I told him, 'Who's Alan Parlor? He will not provide the money—he's just another stooge, just another bill.'"

I took off my fedora and put it down. I removed the scarf mask, shaking out my hair. I pulled off the blonde wig.

"I don't enjoy doing this," I said. "I've had to kill to avenge my husband. I've had to take on another persona, to be someone else. But you, you convinced your husband to kill mine?"

I kneeled down, inches from her, eye to eye.

"They shot him in the face. They shot him in front of my daughter and me. Do you know what that feels like? I was going to leave you for the mob. I was going to leave you to be terrified by them, but no, I said no. I wasn't sure I could kill you. You're not one of the goons. You're not one of his people. You are his wife, a place that should be off-limits, but you're not, are you? You're actually part of it, and you convinced him to kill Alan.

"My name is not Jac Moonshine. My name is Debbie Parlor, and you are going to pay for what you did."

I reached out with my hand, grabbing her throat. I squeezed, bringing my second hand around to assist. As she choked, coughed, and gasped for air, I felt my fingernails dig into her neck, and I didn't care. All I saw was someone who had hurt me beyond measure.

"You killed Alan," I said, at first quietly, then over again. "You killed Alan. You killed Alan."

I could have snapped her neck. I know how to do that, but I didn't. I watched her shake. I watched her body shut down. I watched her die slowly, uncomfortably, fighting for air that would not come. Then I took my hands off and watched her fall to the ground.

I stayed looking at her for about a minute, shaking like I was standing in the artic. I'd killed the goons that night with no hesitation, no afterthought. But this was me that did this. This wasn't my alter ego. I killed her, and I wanted to, almost needed to. Right then, I hated Randazzo not simply for killing my husband, not simply for bringing my girl into a world that was making her like them, but for destroying Debbie.

I put my wig back on, along with the mask and hat, because Jac would have to clean up. I took the body and left it in the middle of the estate, complete with a bottle of hootch labeled with Jac Moonshine. I set her car on fire before I rode off on my bike and placed a phone call to Detective Frogg.

It all went rather smoothly when she was dead. I knew what I was doing. I knew how to play it. Only when I got back that night, only when Debbie came back to the fore, did I shake. What was I now? What had I become? I needed to end this fast. I needed to end this and get out quickly, taking Kelly with me.

When I reached my bedroom, I looked at the duvet pulled back over the bed, two pillows on either side. There was no Alan. I hoped Randazzo would feel this way, too.

Chapter 23

I wasn't up too early that morning, tired after the night before, and to be honest, the entire scene was running through my mind. I could see her face as I choked her, but it wasn't bothering me she was dead, more the way I did it. It became personal. It became about me, not about Jac, not about this other figure I'd created. This figure that would terrify, this otherness. Instead, it became personal, and that scared me.

I sat that morning in my dressing gown and flipped on the news. It was all over the local stations. Berlin Street, three people dead on the estate, not just dead, three people who had been tortured and then hanged as a demonstration to everyone else.

Randazzo's men had been there. Of course, it didn't say it was him, but the newspaper reporter said that a note had been left pinned to one body demanding that Jac Moonshine show herself; otherwise, more bodies would follow.

I felt hollow to the core. Those three people, they had done nothing. Those three people were just being used as bait for me. I had poked the bear with a stick and the bear had reacted in a terrible fashion. I was feeling weak, feeling hollow from what I'd done, but this totally knocked me for six.

I was glued to the television, unable to move, my coffee going cold until Kelly came down the stairs. She put her arm around me, kissed me, and then asked if I wanted my coffee replaced. When I didn't answer, I could hear the concern in her voice.

"Mom, I said, do you want more coffee? Are you okay? Why are you looking at . . ?" She realized. "That was you, wasn't it?" she asked.

"No, that wasn't me leaving those poor people up there. That's Randazzo who has done that," I said. "He's done it because his wife is dead. His wife ordered, or rather convinced him, that your father should be killed, and I choked the life out of her last night."

"Well, good riddance," said Kelly.

"No, Kelly. I choked the life out of her, not Jac Moonshine, me, and now it's all kicked off. He's had enough. He's killing innocent people. He's trying to flush me out. It's coming to a head, Kelly, and there's nowhere left to go. If I walk away, more people will die. So, I have to finish Randazzo, and on his terms, not somewhere quiet now."

"Then I'll come help you," said Kelly. I looked at her face and knew that she meant it.

"No, you can't. You can't. You'll be a liability. You'll be . . ."

"Eamon will help us. Eamon knows what to do. He can handle a gun. I can handle a gun or go with a knife or something. You can't go in alone."

"I have to, Kelly. Don't you get that? I must. Get changed. We're going to the safe house. You're going to stay there with Eamon. If this goes wrong, I have money. The two of you can run."

"No," said Kelly. "You're not. Let's just run."

"No, those people," I said, "those people he butchered, they're on me. Get changed. I've got work to do."

She stormed off, raging at me, but she got dressed and together we drove to the safe house. She stood and watched me get dressed, donning my wig, my fedora, my scarf, my black garb, ready to take the motorbike out for possibly the last time.

I told Eamon if it all went wrong, there was a bag of money at the back of my upstairs' room for him to take. There was also another one for Deck and they were all to scarper as far away as possible. They weren't to come after me. After making them promise to do that, I turned to take the steps down to the bike. Kelly grabbed my arm.

"You don't have to do this. I want you, not Jac. I want you. I need my mom. I've lost my father."

"You'll be fine," I said. "Sit tight. I might even come back."

I heard her cry as I took the steps down to the bike in the cellar. As I rode it up from the basement, I stopped across from Deck and simply gave him a nod. I hadn't told him anything, but I wondered how he would cope if I didn't come through. There was no time to think like that. I opened the throttle, rode out of the building and out onto the street.

Randazzo's building was impressive, in the posh part of town, with a wide expanse of greenery around it. However, the hive of activity that I'd first seen when I'd started watching him was now diminished. Through the gang war, and because of my own actions, he'd lost a lot of men. He was a shell of what he'd been before, and I found it easy to park a little distance from the perimeter and jump the fence into the gardens.

The lack of people was staggering. I stole my way round to a large drawing room on the northwest corner of the building. A guard stood outside but fell with some quick shots from my silenced handgun. There was one goon inside who I stole up on and broke the neck of before he even realized I was there.

Slowly, I crept through the house. I counted another four of the goons I took out as I worked my way towards the central study. I opened the heavy wooden door and saw him behind a large desk.

Randazzo had his back to me, but I recognized the head and the bulk of the man in the seat. Slowly, I raised my gun. This would be it. This would be the revenge complete. This would be me finished. How easy had it been? Too easy!

Something hit me on the side of the neck. Almost instantly, I felt woozy. I went to fire the gun, but someone hit my arm. The gun fell, and I was driven to the ground. It should have been sore, but my senses were all awry.

I'm not sure how long it was before I woke up. The gun was gone, my hat and scarf were gone, the wig was gone, lying in the corner and I realized it, so were my clothes. I sat huddled inside what was a cage, except it was small. I couldn't stretch my feet out; instead, it felt like I was in a dog cage.

One goon realized I had woken, and they took me from the cage, hanging me up in my bare state by my wrists.

Randazzo strode into the windowless room. There were no windows, only bright lights. This was a kill room, a place made for dispatching people with no evidence kept and easy to clean.

He didn't speak, instead he hit me, repeatedly punching me. Sometimes he struck my face, sometimes the stomach, the ribs, sometimes, just anywhere. Then there was a stick, knotted and jaggy. Satisfied I had been truly battered, he left me for his goons to throw me back in the cage.

It was maybe an hour after that he came to the cage, and he told me he would let the boys in. They all wanted to have a go at me. They all had friends I had removed. Inside, I was quaking, but I didn't let him see that.

"Where's Kelly?"

I spat in his face. "Far away," I mumbled.

"I see where she gets it from," he said. "I understand now. Like you, someone who doesn't know their place. I'd have looked after you," he said. "I have many such women set up. There are several women like you should have been. I visit them, they keep me entertained and they have a good life. You could have had it too. Instead, look at you, you'll be treated like a dog now, and then like a dog you'll be put down, Kelly too. I'm going to go after her."

"She's gone." I said and laughed hysterically, though there was no good reason behind it. I hoped she'd gone. I'd left the money for her and Eamon.

"You trusted him because you'd saved him. You think people reciprocate. Well, they don't. You must own people," said Randazzo.

My heart sank. He was talking about Eamon. Did he actually own Eamon? Or had Eamon buckled, his passion for Kelly cooled.

"Just because you do something good doesn't mean they'll do anything for you. Berlin Street didn't come to your rescue, did they? They didn't say, 'Don't you bother going, we'll come. We'll sort him out,' and you actually trusted Eamon O'Reilly."

My heart went cold and out of my cage, I saw Eamon walking into the room holding Kelly at gunpoint. She had a black eye and a cut lip.

"Good job. You see, this is the thing," Randazzo said, pointing at Kelly and then looking back at me. "Eamon here, he upset me. Eamon was not in my good books, but he brings me gifts, a gift like this so he can go because that's what people want. They're not loyal, they see what's best for them and they do it. Any problems bringing her in?" asked Randazzo motioning towards Kelly's blackeye.

"Oh, she's frisky," said Eamon, "but I can handle her."

I kicked the cage, but it wasn't open. Randazzo called his men into the room. I saw three of them. He opened my cage and reached in, pulling me out. My hands were tied behind my back, and I looked a mess, like some street wench from the fifteenth century.

"Shall I make her like you?" asked Randazzo, laughing. "I should have the two of you like this. I think not," he said, "because I'm generous. I understand why she would want to kill me; I understand why she would want to go after all my men. It should be admired, wanting revenge like she does. I'll kill her first, straight and simple."

I kicked out but was held in place. Inside, tears were welling up and my frustration was overcoming me. I was desperate.

"In fact, Eamon here can do it just to show you what people are like. My men told me she had a thing for him. Well, he had nothing for her. You'll understand that, sweetheart."

Randazzo put his hand up, taking Kelly's chin in his hand. "You're skank to him, just a piece of meat to be used. Oh, Eamon, you can do it from behind. She doesn't need to be looking at you. Least we can do for her; better than her father got."

Kelly snarled. I went to kick out, but I got held back, one goon at each of my arms, and Randazzo came across and slapped me hard.

"You just stand there and take it," he said. "You stand there and watch."

He even pushed Kelly down onto her knees. She looked across at me. At first, I thought she would be brave, not showing any sort of panic. Her head had been bowed, but now she stared up at me.

Kelly, from childhood, always could lift me with a smile. Kids do that. Kids have this thing where they can connect with you when you know their little grins, not the big cheesy ones they put on for people, but the little self-satisfaction grins. The edges of Kelly's mouth were curling up. Her eyes were not soulless, not hollow. They were on fire. I braced myself. Randazzo looked at me and laughed.

"Enjoy this," he said as he turned back to Kelly. Eamon raised his gun and from three feet away, he shot Randazzo between the eyes. I wasn't looking when the gunshot went off. Instead, I had kicked one man beside me, hard into the kneecaps. When I connected, I performed the same action with my other foot to my other captor.

Kelly was up off her knees, throwing herself into one of Randazzo's goons. One beside me suddenly fell to the ground as another shot rang out. The other beside me, moaning from my attack, grabbed me, but I back-butted, driving my head up into his nose. It became a bloody mess, and I turned and kicked him, letting him tumble to the floor.

Eamon, standing across from me, fired a couple of shots into him while I ran over to Kelly. She had gone down to the ground with the man, who was now putting his arms around her neck, trying to throw her off. I dove to the ground with both knees, smashing straight into his face.

"Get clear!" shouted Eamon. I rolled away, watched him throw Kelly out of the way and fire two more shots.

"Free your mom," Eamon said. Kelly produced a knife and

cut the bonds behind me. She then pointed over to my clothing while Eamon stood guard at the door. There were no cameras in the room, nothing to record evidence. Eamon stood and kept watch before telling me that someone was coming.

"It's normal for him to send people away, especially when something like this is happening," he said, "but I saw another two on the way in. One's coming down the corridor now. We'll need to get the other."

My limbs were aching, but I felt good. I felt like I could go another mile. Clearly, I didn't look good, though. There was dried blood around my face. There were cuts and bruises like never before all over me, but none of that mattered now. Now we had to get out.

We spread out to the walls as the door opened and the man Eamon had been talking about walked in. He dispatched him with ease. I took the man's gun, and we tore out of the room. There was someone getting into a car in the driveway, and we ran over, firing at the car. We peppered it. I checked and saw the man was dead in the car.

"Let's go," said Eamon, but I shook my head.

"Let's go to the garage. Let's set this place a blaze."

There needed to be a mark. There needed to be something to show the city the man's fall. I sent Eamon and Kelly back in while I guarded the grounds. They found gasoline in the garage and got to work pouring it while I took a spade. In the beautifully manicured lawn, I dug out the letters JAC. This was important. Everyone needed to know who had won.

The blaze had started by the time the cops arrived because they didn't race to a house like this too quickly. We were over the rear fence and back at the safe house by the time the news was covering what had happened. I'd like to say I felt good. I'd like to say I was a better person because of all of this, but I felt sore, and I felt hollow, and I wondered what would be next.

But Randazzo was dead!

Chapter 24

You're probably expecting an epilogue. Well, the short version is I took an awful long time to recover from the beating of my life. When I got home, Kelly called the emergency services saying I had fainted and tumbled down the stairs. There was a possibility of broken ribs, and when we went to the hospital, they did indeed show up several hairline fractures. My leg too also had severe trauma along it.

The doctor questioned the fall, but I said I couldn't have any kickback because of who had done this. He understood a battered woman who couldn't talk and simply treated me, although he was shocked at my injuries.

The result was a lot of rest and the chance to see developments from a bed. I saw reruns of Randazzo's house burning down. I saw many on the TV saying how glad they were he was gone, but I wondered would anybody else fill the void. Donovan was still there. Would he take over the drug dealers? Did somebody else step in when Kozlov was killed? I wasn't about cleaning up the town; I was about avenging my husband. Things had escalated quickly towards the end, and I was just happy that I'd put an end to it.

Kelly came up to visit me, along with Eamon. I didn't like

them together. As a mother, the last type of person I wanted her to be involved with was Eamon and yet he had stuck with her. He had shot Randazzo for me. He'd risked his neck coming to get me.

I guess I'd spared his life too, though. I had stopped him from being taken out by Randazzo's thugs, but what I had done was not an act of kindness; it was simply putting him in a position where I could use him. It felt a bit off he had simply done it for his girl. His "girl." I'm finding that hard to live with, but I guess when I look at it, she's like me. I never thought of Alan as a crook.

Alan looked after the legitimate affairs of Randazzo, but he knew fine rightly what the man was; he knew how the man worked. The money that was used to pay for the legal side of Randazzo's dealings came from terrible places.

I remember being back in the nightclub, dancing on the stage in front of them. I wondered how many of the girls around me chose to work there. How many were high, feeding their drug habit with what they earned there? There was certainly nothing wholesome about it. Kelly had chosen Eamon, but thankfully, he seems to be not too bad an egg, and he certainly looks after her.

It took me a while to get out of hospital and truthfully, I enjoyed it. Things were quiet. I sent Kelly down to make sure Deck was okay. Something told me not to sell the place and to keep the motorbike stashed away.

Deck enjoyed it. He had a roof over his head, he had food brought to him. He even had his drugs, and I doubted he would tell on his landlord.

Kelly seemed a little lost, as did I. All our anger had been poured towards Randazzo and his men; now they were gone.

I'd like to say that there was a satisfaction in it, but there wasn't. Eamon had been the one to kill him. We hadn't even had the chance to see terror in his eyes, hadn't had the chance to see him panic. I think the closest he got to that was sorrow. Maybe he understood my sorrow, not that it made him repent.

Kelly moved out and took up a flat with Eamon. which I think is a good thing. The two of us had a lot to talk about—too much, and we needed distance. Eamon, when I came over, would go out. Kelly came to see me often in the first three weeks of my return home due to how I felt. The pain was still strong, but she started to get her own life and I got back to mine. No one knew who Jac Moonshine was, and Jac faded into the background. Like I said, I wasn't there to avenge the city; there was no hero clearing it up. I was there to exact revenge on those who had killed my husband, and that had been done.

I eventually went back to my martial arts, and I had a busy schedule. I enjoy playing tennis with the girls in the summer, attending this party, that, out to shows. I had the money, you see.

Alan had left a hole, and I was not inclined to simply sit down, but in truth, I was hollow. I wanted to be at these things with him; that's why I did it, you see—that's why I accepted being his woman at home. That's why I was the perfect little wife when the likes of Randazzo and his kind came round. I was there for Alan. I missed my partner. That ultimately was the problem, not the fact that there were others still alive. I know that now. They are dead and it doesn't help.

It was over six months later, with my life back in full swing, that I received a knock at the door. I hadn't long come in from my gym training and I opened the door in my leggings and tracksuit top to a suddenly taken aback Detective Frogg.

"I'm sorry to bother you," he said. "I can come back if there's a better time."

Something inside me was kicking. Something inside me was wondering why he was here. Had something trailed back from Jac Moonshine? I still had the bottles, I still had the bike, the wig, everything else, but nothing in the house. It was all at the hide, so what could he possibly want?

"I don't know if you want to know this," he said, "but I'd like to talk a little about your husband's killing again. I have a few more details. I'm not sure you'll want to know, but if you do, I'm happy to come in and talk. We found something out, you see."

My curiosity was piqued, and I opened the door, leading him inside. I was the perfect host, popping to the kitchen, making coffee, bringing it back inside, and then sitting opposite him. He watched the room like a detective, wondering why each piece of furniture, each picture, was there, and I could tell he was soaking it in, allowing it to infuse into his brain to see what he could concoct from it.

"We've just been fed some information from another case. Your husband's murder came up, and a lowlife told me it was sanctioned by a Mr. Aldridge. Are you aware of Mr. Aldridge?"

Well, I wasn't. Randazzo was the top dog, as far as I knew.

"I'm sorry, detective, but I've never heard of Mr. Aldridge. Randazzo, yes, he came here after the funeral. He tried to . . . well, make me a whore on the side, but somebody took care of that for me.

The man coughed. "Somebody we have yet to find," he said. "I just thought I'd let you know it was Mr. Aldridge that gave the go-ahead. He's quite a bigwig, but he's not from Mannersberg.

More of a bigger picture man, Randazzo's boss. He'll be putting somebody else in here, no doubt."

"Just for completeness," I said, "can you tell me what it was he actually did? You said he sanctioned it—in what way?"

"Well, Randazzo went to him because Alan was sanctioned originally by Mr. Aldridge as well. Everyone that Randazzo brought in, they all ran past Aldridge's eyes, and I believe Aldridge was quite fond of your husband. There was talk one day that he may even be moved up to Mr. Aldridge, if his firm could handle it."

"That's news to me," I said.

"Just understand me; this Aldridge was the one who killed your husband. He was the one that insisted on the Kozlov connection being kept. He might as well have pulled the trigger."

I stood up, walked over to the window, and stared out at a street that was quiet. The school day was not yet over. I saw sprinklers sending water over gardens; I saw people washing cars, the odd person walking their dog. Everything was calm, everything.

"How did this man know who spoke to you?" I asked.

"He's a lowlife. Aldridge threatened him, threatened him by telling him Alan's story. That's what the likes of Aldridge will do. If there's somebody they need to pull into line, they'll recount what they did to someone else. Of course, it's a tale, not a confession. That's what your husband's become," said Frogg. "He's become a lesson for the rest of those who would dare challenge Aldridge's crew."

I felt a shiver run down me. I walked over, picked up my cup and took it to the coffee jug and poured myself some more. I gulped it, all the time visible to the ever-steady gaze of

Detective Frogg.

"Still, the ones who pulled the trigger, Jac Moonshine's did for them."

"Yes," I replied, "yes, of course. Of course. All behind me now. Thank you for coming, Detective Frogg, but I think it's a wasted journey. I need to keep all these past things from me. It's all behind me, all the stuff that . . . well, that it's not healthy to reflect on."

"No, it's not," said Frogg. "Here, a little memento, maybe an item to show closure. One of the things from the Randazzo house crime scene, probably fitting that you should have it, now it's come out of evidence."

He handed me over a small bottle of hooch with Jac Moonshine written on the side. Eamon must have taken it with him when they rescued me. I took it off him, placed it on the table.

"She really did clear things up for us," I said. "But I need no more favors. Alan left us with plenty of money. Thank you for coming around, Detective Frogg, but it's probably really not something I needed to know. Thank you for your time."

He stood up and shook my hand, advising me if there was anything more, I should get in touch. He stopped on the doorstep, turned to me, and said, "I think I saw your daughter with Eamon O'Rourke. Might not be the best connection for the family."

I simply nodded, opened the door, and waved goodbye to the detective. I shut it, turned, and placed my back on the door. Somebody was still alive. Aldridge was the one who had said it. All the pain had left me hollow, but now it was like that hollow was being filled in again. I was back with purpose. Aldridge was the next step. Aldridge would need taking down. Aldridge!

I guess that's your prologue right there. Aldridge. They've done it once. Why couldn't they do it again? That's when I realized. The thing about revenge is it's open-ended. Nothing is ever quite enough.

I checked outside, making sure Frogg had gone, before I grabbed my jacket and stepped into the car. Soon I entered the safe house and gave Deck a nod. He said he hadn't seen me for a while, the best part of four months, but I wasn't there for small talk, and I went upstairs to the computer. As I sat and typed "Aldridge," I felt like there were two people in the seat. "Come on, girl," said a voice inside my head. "Jac's right with you. Let's bring this home."

Read on to discover the Patrick Smythe series!

READ ON TO DISCOVER THE PATRICK SMYTHE SERIES!

Patrick Smythe is a former Northern Irish policeman who

after suffering an amputation after a bomb blast, takes to the sea between the west coast of Scotland and his homeland to ply his trade as a private investigator. Join Paddy as he tries to work to his own ethics while knowing how to bend the rules he once enforced. Working from his beloved motorboat 'Craigantlet', Paddy decides to rescue a drug mule in this short story from the pen of G R Jordan.

Join G R Jordan's monthly newsletter about forthcoming releases and special writings for his tribe of avid readers and then receive your free Patrick Smythe short story.

Go to https://bit.ly/PatrickSmythe for your Patrick Smythe journey to start!

About the Author

GR Jordan is a self-published author who finally decided at forty that in order to have an enjoyable lifestyle, his creative beast within would have to be unleashed. His books mirror that conflict in life where acts of decency contend with self-promotion, goodness stares in horror at evil, and kindness blindsides us when we at our worst. Corrupting our world with his parade of wondrous and horrific characters, he highlights everyday tensions with fresh eyes whilst taking his methodical, intelligent mainstays on a roller-coaster ride of dilemmas, all the while suffering the banter of their provocative sidekicks.

A graduate of Loughborough University where he masqueraded as a chemical engineer but ultimately played American football, Gary had worked at changing the shape of cereal flakes and pulled a pallet truck for a living. Watching vegetables freeze at -40'C was another career highlight and he was also one of the Scottish Highlands "blind" air traffic controllers.

These days he has graduated to answering a telephone to people in trouble before telephoning other people to sort it out.

Having flirted with most places in the UK, he is now based in the Isle of Lewis in Scotland where his free time is spent between raising a young family with his wife, writing, figuring out how to work a loom and caring for a small flock of chickens. Luckily, his writing is influenced by his varied work and life experience as the chickens have not been the poetical inspiration he had hoped for!

You can connect with me on:

https://grjordan.com

https://facebook.com/carpetlessleprechaun

Subscribe to my newsletter:

https://bit.ly/PatrickSmythe

Also by G R Jordan

G R Jordan writes across multiple genres including crime, dark and action adventure fantasy, feel good fantasy, mystery thriller and horror fantasy. Below is a selection of his work. Whilst all books are available across online stores, signed copies are available at his personal shop.

Jac for the People

https://grjordan.com/product/jac-for-the-people

Her husband's true killer still walks. A new love means a quieter approach to revenge. But will the cries of a neighborhood bring Jac back to the fore?

When Debbie sets off for the city of Dawn to hunt down the man who ordered her husband's death, she finds a new champion and love in its midst. Together they mount a campaign for justice against the crime lord but when Debbie sees the despair of the innocent in a neighborhood being used for greed and corruption, Jac rears her head again. Can Debbie marry Jac to herself and become a true arbiter of justice? Or will Jac deal with the corruption in her own inimitable way?

Get on board with this tongue-in-cheek revenge thriller that will make you question just what lives inside you when the anger is stirred. Hey, you might even find it more fun than you are!

Highlands & Islands Detective Thrillers

https://grjordan.com/product/waters-edge

Join stalwart DI Macleod and his burgeoning new DC McGrath as they look into the darker side of the stunningly scenic and wilder parts of the north of Scotland. From the Black Isle to Lewis, from Mull to Harris and across to the small Isles, the Uists and Barra, this mismatched pairing follow murders, thieves and vengeful victims in an effort to restore tranquillity to the remoter parts of the land.

Be part of this tale of a surprise partnership amidst the foulest deeds and darkest souls who stalk this peaceful and most beautiful of lands, and you'll never see the Highlands the same way again.

Kirsten Stewart Thrillers

https://grjordan.com/product/a-shot-at-democracy

Join Kirsten Stewart on a shadowy ride through the underbelly of the Highlands of Scotland where among the beauty and splendour of the majestic landscape lies corruption and intrigue to match any city. From murders to extortion, missing children to criminals operating above the law, the Highland former detective must learn a tougher edge to her work as she puts her own life on the line to protect those who cannot defend themselves.

Having left her beloved murder investigation team far behind, Kirsten has to battle personal tragedy and loss while adapting to a whole new way of executing her duties where your mistakes are your own. As Kirsten comes to terms with working with the new team, she often operates as the groups solo field agent, placing herself in danger and trouble to rescue those caught on the dark side of life. With action packed scenes and tense scenarios of murder and greed, the Kirsten Stewart thrillers will have you turning page after page to see your favourite Scottish lass home!

There's life after Macleod, but a whole new world of death!

The Disappearance of Russell Hadleigh (Patrick Smythe Book 1)
https://grjordan.com/product/the-disappearance-of-russell-hadleigh
A retired judge fails to meet his golf partner. His wife calls for help while running a fantasy play ring. When Russians start co-opting into a fairly-traded clothing brand, can Paddy untangle the strands before the bodies start littering the golf course?

In his first full novel, Patrick Smythe, the single-armed former policeman, must infiltrate the golfing social scene to discover the fate of his client's husband. Assisted by a young starlet of the greens, Paddy tries to understand just who bears a grudge and who likes to play in the rough, culminating in a high stakes showdown where lives are hanging by the reaction of a moment. If you love pacey action, suspicious motives and devious characters, then Paddy Smythe operates amongst your kind of people.

Love is a matter of taste but money always demands more of its suitor.

Printed in Great Britain
by Amazon

33645887R00128